Pianissimo

by

Lauren Shiro

Vanilla Heart Publishing
USA

Pianissimo
by Lauren Shiro

Copyright 2014 Lauren Shiro

Published by: Vanilla Heart Publishing
www.VanillaHeartBooksAndAuthors.com
10121 Evergreen Way, 25-156
Everett, WA 98204 USA

This book is a work of fiction. Names, characters, places, and incidents are either the product of the author's imagination or are used fictitiously, and any resemblance to places, events, or persons living or dead is purely coincidental.

ISBN-13: 9780692310816 ISBN-10: 0692310819

10 9 8 7 6 5 4 3 2 1 First Edition

First Printing, October 2014
Printed in the United States of America

Pianissimo

by

Lauren Shiro

Table of Contents

Dedication

Discussion Starters

More Great Books by Lauren Shiro

Lauren Shiro Author Bio and Photo

Dedication

This book is dedicated to all of the brave members of the LGBT community who have come before us. All of the heroes who worked diligently that we might all have equal rights and status. From the very famed to the unknown, their sacrifice and work has blessed and benefitted us all. For that, I am thankful.

Prologue

It was a chilly early spring day in Manhattan. The morning sky was painted in various shades of grey as a light mist sprinkled the city. The sun wasn't visible, but there was a bright spot where the clouds appeared weak and thin. This was going to turn into a beautiful day, Harold just knew it.

He walked into the factory to start yet another day – a day just like any other. Yet he knew that today was special, too. He loved his life, he loved the Spring, and he loved his job. Though he may never meet any of them, he knew that his work touched the lives of many, many people.

Harold walked to the back of the factory and hung up his long brown rain coat. He was the first one in, which was fairly common for him. There was something about the silence and solitude of the large building that fed his excitement even further. He deeply inhaled. He loved the smell of wood. Perfect, beautiful silence, and the intoxicating smell of lumber. This was indeed a wonderful day!

Harold smiled to himself. Although this was an ordinary day for him, he knew that this was an extraordinary day for someone else. Another person would be touched by his work today.

He walked over to his current project. A blank canvas for music. This piano had yet to be finished, let alone yet to be played. The mahogany wood looked and smelled exquisite. He closed his eyes, imaging this perfect piano. It was strong and sturdy, beautiful and classic. The wood was pristine, the music from the keys was competition for the singing angels in Heaven. Oh what a work of art this will be!

His daydream went further. Who would play it? Would it be a personal piece for a family to enjoy? Would a future professional pianist learn on it? Would it be used on a grander scale? What kind of music would be played on it? The possibilities were endless! This piano that he has built with his own two hands has a future greater than he could ever try to imagine. He smiled with pride and excitement. The infinite possibilities: that was why Harold loved his job.

He ran his hand over the smooth mahogany wood. It was no small feat to create a piano, and this one was no different. It had taken well over a year to get to this point. This instrument was to be perfect, and he would ensure that it was. After all this time, this blank canvas would be completed and then released into the world soon. How very exciting!

There was no need to wait for his co-workers. He just began doing what he did best: building pianos. He gently grabbed the sound board and carefully lowered it into the case. He lowered the harp on top of it, grabbed some string and began stringing it.

Today was going to be an absolutely wonderful day! His next masterpiece would be complete so that both he and someone else could enjoy it for years to come.

Chapter One

Corinne sat in the bare living room with the front door to the old house wide open. The screen door made a pitiful barrier between her and the raging thunderstorm outside. The light, sweet, crisp scent of rain tickled the back of her nostrils with each gust of wind. The rain was more than welcome, though. The humidity had finally died down and there was even a slight chill in the air. Drenched green leaves danced and twirled on just the other side of the door.

Surrounding Corinne was a sea of boxes. Her whole life was contained in the plain brown parcels. Pictures, memories, books, sentimental items: indeed, her entire existence was covered in bubble wrap and contained in the boxes she had clearly marked.

It was ironic, really, that she sat alone in the big, old, empty house. She and Darryl had just purchased the historic home and with impeccable timing, he was sent off one final time. After so many years, she should be used to military life, but it never really got any easier.

She sat in dark silence, simply listening to the rain and thunder until the storm finally passed.

The new washer and dryer had finally arrived after a week without the necessary appliances. Excited to finally start living like a person in the twenty-first century, Corinne ran to the old outside basement doors for the workers to unload the machines.

The rust was so thick, she couldn't open them. She pulled and pulled with all her might. Nothing. The doors seemed to be rusted shut. Now what was she going to do? The delivery guys were going to be here in just a few minutes, and they needed some way to get them down there. She thought and thought. Was there a way to break up the rust? There was so much on there, it acted like a sealant. But did rust work that way? Could you break up rust? She had no idea, but she had to try something – anything!

She ran back into the house and looked through the box that was labeled "tools." She pushed and moved everything around. This was Darryl's domain. Why couldn't he be there to help?

After sifting through the box for a few minutes, she took a hammer and a flat-head screw driver, and ran back outside.

She faced the doors again. She pushed the screw driver into the rust with all of her strength. Pieces began to chip off. In some of the bigger areas, she pounded on the screw driver with a hammer. She hit and chiseled for quite a while. She gave the doors one last pull and they finally opened.

Curious, Corinne walked in; the service men weren't here yet. She hadn't been down here before. It was probably a good idea that she gets somewhat familiar with it before they arrive.

She brushed the cobwebs off her face as she slowly entered the dark mysterious basement. She finally found a light switch in the shadows. After a couple of flickers, the light finally stayed on. The basement was simple. Antiquated rocks and plaster formed the walls. The ceiling was low, reminding her of her height. She looked around. There were the normal pipes, electrical box and the usual odds and ends one would expect with an older basement.

As she peered around the corner, something green caught her eye. Slowly, the form took shape from under the shadows. It was an old piano. A very old piano. As Corinne stepped closer, she read a large brass plate that still sat regally on the old instrument. R. S. Howard. It was an R. S. Howard upright piano. The backboard was missing, exposing the scrawny, naked strings and hammers. A few of the keys were permanently depressed. The piano's original rich wood finish was hidden under an old coat of drab olive green paint.

Why on earth was there a piano in the basement? Who keeps a piano down there? It's an unfinished basement. It's not like people would be entertaining company in this hole. It was so weird.

And why was it painted? Who would paint a piano? Especially such an ugly color. It looked stupid.

Corinne just shook her head in confusion.

As she stared at the old instrument, memories of her musical days came flooding back to her. She remembered the years and years of piano lessons. She remembered all the recitals and concerts. She smiled reflecting back on all those great memories.

She walked over to it. She could only imagine the beautiful music that had once been played on the old piece. She softly touched it. A burst of a cold sensation struck her hand and raced up her arm. Corinne immediately dropper her hand. The cold feeling was gone.

She was struck by a burst of energy while she continued to stare at the piano.

"Hello?" A man's voice echoed down the stairs.

Corinne turned around "Oh hi! Come on down here. The hook ups are..." Her eyes darted around the room, trying to find the connectors for the machines. There! She found them. "They're over here!"

"Okay! Thank you."

Corinne stepped away from the piano so she would be out of the workmen's way. She watched them work, but she was also strangely pulled to look at the piano as well.

Corinne carefully guided the brush through her fine, and very tangled hair. Her sand colored locks seemed more chocolaty brown at the moment. Her hair always looked so much darker after she showered. As she stared at herself in the mirror, she noticed small drops of paint still remained on her face. How was that possible? She had scrubbed herself raw in the shower.

"Ugh," she said to herself. She decided to leave it be. "It's not like anyone is going to see me any way."

She continued to brush the knots out of her hair. She stared deeply into her own brown eyes.

She could hear her brother Evan now. "Look at you! You have more paint on yourself than you got on the walls! You don't know what you're doing. Leave that stuff to the guys. We know what we're doing, and we won't make nearly the mess you made! You'd better go shower again!" Then she heard his mean, hurtful laugh. Why were her bothers always so nasty and cruel like that? They never let her do anything. And when she did – like she's been doing here – all they ever did was mock her.

15

Pianissimo

She did alright. The house was coming together slowly, but it was coming together. She's trying to take care of an entire house completely by herself! She had done an okay job painting.

Hadn't she? There was still paint in her hair and on her face. Evan was right.

"Oh why do I bother, anyway?!" She shouted. Corinne ran and flopped herself dejectedly onto her bed and simply wept.

Chapter Two

Corinne lay quietly in her large, empty bed. The new bedroom was still too new, too foreign...too empty. Corinne longed for the familiarity of Darryl's scent; for his warm body hogging up the majority of the bed; for even his snore.

She lay in the bed staring at the ceiling, her mind focused on her absent husband when a loud, undistinguishable noise startled her. It wasn't a crash, perhaps more like a bang. It was loud, whatever it was, and it was concerning. What could have caused such a noise? Did something break? Is the house falling apart? Please don't let it be anything big, I'm too stressed right now. I can't take anything more! She prayed.

Corinne got up and ran downstairs to see what had happened. Corinne went from room to room, turning on the lights, exploring each area very carefully. Nothing was out of place. Everything looked fine. Nothing was broken. Maybe she just imagined it.

When every room on the first floor had been checked, she debated if she should go back up to bed, or check out the basement. She wasn't a big fan of the basement. It was dark, dank, and kind of creepy.

Something had fallen or something happened. She needed to see what had happened. She couldn't rest until she knew everything was really okay.

She finally let herself down into the basement through the interior entrance. The old wooden door needed some coaxing in order to open. With a gentle push from her hip, the door opened and Corinne carefully managed the old staircase.

As she surveyed the room, nothing seemed out of order. Nothing was broken; nothing had crashed to the floor. All the various boxes, appliances and potpourri remained in their original positions. Confused, Corinne looked a little deeper into the room and found the girls laying on the piano.

"Oh girls!" She said as she scooped up her two cats.

Millie and Mollie, her two feline sisters who were notorious for getting into trouble had done just that. They had been hiding since the move.

When they first got there, Corinne had placed a litter box in the basement, and another in the first floor bathroom. She kept their food and water dishes full in the kitchen.

Thankfully, they had found the litter boxes and the food and water.

After days of hiding, they had decided to explore tonight...and their curiosity had clearly gotten the best of them. One – or maybe both - of them must have landed on some keys when they jumped on to the archaic apparatus.

With one cat in each arm, she went back upstairs to hopefully get some rest.

Corinne paced around the kitchen. Finally! She answered.

"Hello?"

"Hey Rach! It's Corinne."

"Hey!" Rachel replied excitedly. "So how's it going?" Her warm, familiar voice was comforting to Corinne.

"Ugh. Alright, I suppose." Corinne answered. "It's not easy doing all this by myself."

"I know, sweetie. Darryl'll be home soon. You've done it before; you're strong enough to do it again."

"Thanks. It's just...it's just so different from Nellis. The people here are different. I don't even sound like them – I talk different. I feel like I'm such an outsider. That I'm weird. I just feel so alone." Softly, Corinne began to sob.

"Oh honey," Rachel said. "I'm sorry. Have you tried reaching out to meet other wives?"

"We're not on base," Corinne sniffled. "I feel so far away from everyone and everything. I..."

Rachel remind silent, but supportive. "Honey, you know where to go and who to call. I wish I was there to help you out. But I can't, I'm out here. You just need to reach out to the community there. You'll find friends, I'm sure."

Corinne took a deep breath. "Yeah, I know you're right."

"Now, tell me something good about life out there." Rachel said, hoping to perk up her friend's spirits.

Corinne stopped to think for a moment. She hesitated to speak. "It's...big. The girls like it here. There's room for them to run and play and hide...especially on the piano."

"What piano?"

"Oh, there's an old piano in the basement and they love to just jump on it in the middle of the night and hit all the keys and create a lovely ruckus."

"Oh, nice. I see they're being incredibly considerate of you, as usual." Rachel teased. She paused and took a deep breath. "Look, honey. I know this is tough. You have to hang in there, okay? You can get through this. Darryl will be home soon and that old house will soon be your home, okay?"

"Okay," Corinne answered through both the tears and a weak smile.

A tall, thin woman stood in the dark, her arm rested heavily on some kind of ledge – perhaps a bureau or other piece of furniture. It was too dark to tell. The moonlight slithered its way in through the window, shadowing her tall, lean figure on the wall. She didn't move. She couldn't move. Even if she could, she wouldn't want to. The silence pierced her soul. The room sat mute, but the woman seemed tense and overwrought with the noise in her own mind.

Unable to breathe, unable to move, the woman stayed motionless; the furniture was the only thing supporting her.

Corinne woke up from her dream sad and confused. What a haunting image: that woman standing in the dark. Despondency emanated from this woman. Who was she? What did the dream mean?

Slowly rising to face another day of solitude, Corinne tried desperately to shake the heartrending feeling from her dream that still consumed her.

Corinne sat waiting on the wicker chair on the porch. The dark grey sky promised a powerful storm, and it did not disappoint.

Soon, sheets of rain surrounded the porch. Corinne was lightly tickled by some misdirected rain drops. The cool mist chilled her skin. Thunder roared infinitely around her. Bright sudden strikes of lightning lit up the horizon.

It was almost enlivening. Corinne had been feeling so depressed and lonely all day. It seemed that everyone had abandoned her...even God.

Now God was putting on quite a light show, though. At least he hadn't abandoned her completely.

The mist on her skin reminded her that she was alive. She had a life and she needed to live it. Behind her was a home that was all her own. It needed her attention. She hated the solitude of that house. Maybe, just maybe, if she put some of herself into it, she'd get something back.

Corinne sat quietly, taking in nature's light show for a few more minutes.

She could hear one of the cats scratching the door.

"Okay, okay. I'm coming." She stood up and stretched. She looked out at the storm one last time before going back inside.

Corinne brushed the last stroke of paint in the kitchen. Finally, the massive room had been tackled and no longer resembled the kitchen she grew up with in 1974. That loud, awful gold and brown color scheme had now been concealed by a gentle deep red and light cream combination.

She looked around the room. It really was nice. She had done well. The colors gave the room that perfect country Americana look. This was a kitchen she could enjoy and be proud of. Pleased with herself, she wiped away the sweat from her forehead with her arm. Still holding the brush in her right hand, she cautiously stepped down the step-ladder.

At the second to last step, she watched a field mouse scamper across the kitchen floor. Corinne gasped and her heart began to pound in her chest. The little creature ran and crawled into a microscopic hole in the baseboard.

Corinne stood on the step-ladder, trying to catch her breath. After a couple of minutes, she called out, "Darryl!" Her voice merely echoed through the large, empty house. There was no response, nor anyone to respond. "Argh!" She whispered as one lone tear escaped her eyes. "He won't be home soon enough!" Mustering up what courage she could, she stepped down and began to clean up her painting supplies.

The breeze created by folding a towel gently blew back Corinne's hair. She listened to all the various peculiar sounds of the weird old house. Maybe it was the mice in the walls, maybe it was the foundation settling just a little bit more, Corinne didn't know. She just knew that it was a strange house with strange sounds.

This bizarre old house was all she knew here. She had become a prisoner inside its plaster walls. She spent the majority of her time confined within it. When she could escape, Corinne found herself running back to find quiet sanctuary after getting lost in the foreign town. She hated the antiquated building, and yet she would come running back to it. Sick irony.

It was an irony she did not like. She wasn't happy inside the house, but she wasn't happy outside of it, either.

Why couldn't she be back out at Nellis in Las Vegas? A place where she had friends. A city that was vibrant and full of life. And her home there was far better than this old, wretched shack.

Well, maybe it wasn't that bad. It wasn't a shack. It was actually a decent sized house. The biggest she and Darryl ever had. They bought it for its size and charm. There was something to be said for the character of an old farm house. They had a good sized lot too. A nice, quiet field expanded far beyond the house.

It really wasn't bad at all. It was bad because Corinne was alone. She had to manage fixing the house up, learning the new city, taking care of the cats, and taking care of herself. It was overwhelming. There was so much to do. Fixing up the house wasn't just about picking out nice pain colors. There was real work to be done and she didn't know how to do that. She had never painted a house before this, either. The outside world of Louisville was scary, but the needs of the house were even more scary.

Pianissimo

It was really the circumstances: Corinne's situation that was the problem. She was isolated and afraid. The house itself wasn't bad. It was a big, old, interesting building. She was doing the best she could to improve and update it. So really, this anomalous old house was slowly becoming Corinne's home.

Corinne slept lightly. The sun was just beginning to hint at day light. As Corinne's mind swayed between sleep and consciousness, she heard light, beautiful piano music playing. Her almost dream-state of mind was peaceful as she enjoyed the sweet serenade. Corinne's mind focused on nothing, and this tune was the perfect soundtrack.

Soon thereafter, Corinne arose to the light streaming into the large windows of her bedroom. She could still hear the piano producing beautiful music. Corinne quietly hummed a piece of the pleasant melody that had stayed with her from her sleep.

She unknowingly continued to hum the song as she enjoyed her morning coffee on the front porch.

As Corinne carefully navigated the basement stairs with a full laundry basket, she noticed something on the overhead beam she had never seen before.

It was just a wire hung over a nail. She knew that nail had been sticking out of the beam, she had seen it countless times since moving into the old house. She was quite familiar with the old nail. She hadn't seen the wire before, though. Never before did she take notice of a wire being draped over that nail. The wire somehow made its way up there.

But how? She doubted that either of the cats had the dexterity to hang a wire over a nail. It was so odd. It just didn't make sense. She had to assume that her memory was wrong. The wire must have been up there all this time. There was no other logical explanation.

With a huff, she figured it was a sight she had simply missed before; Corinne then went about getting her laundry started.

Chapter Three

Corinne sat and flipped from channel to channel on the large, wall-mounted television. Nothing was entertaining enough. It hadn't been for hours. Television wasn't even numbing her pain and isolation. It just seemed be to be dumb and pointless.

The moonlight trickled in through the thick, leaded glass windows as the hours ticked away. She sighed heavily as she imagined Darryl by her side as they watched a movie together. Just like they used to. She'd curl up next to him, and he even watched her silly romantic comedies. She loved those days and those memories. It was a sweet sentiment. She would give anything to have that again right now.

No matter how hard she wished, Darryl still did not appear. Those days are gone. They are nothing more than memories. Her present life was far from those old, wonderful days. Now she was all alone, and her husband was thousands of miles away. There were no romantic comedies on the screen before her, and there was no one to cuddle with. She was in solitary confinement.

"It's just too lonely." Corinne said.

She heard her statement echo for a few seconds throughout the house. "It's just too lonely" continued to ring in her ears, but the voice wasn't hers. It was the voice of someone different – another woman.

Corinne bent down to take the canister out of the vacuum when something popped out in the corner of her eye. Startled, she turned her eyes towards it. Her heart began to race. Who or what was it? Why was there something there that she had never seen before. She was certain someone had broken into her house. She was petrified. She was out in the open. There was nowhere to run.

This person was there and they had to have some kind of motive. Who else would break into an old house where a single woman lived? What was their motive? Was it money for drugs? Was he a rapist? Some psychopathic killer?

Her heart began to race even more. Beads of sweat built up at her hair line. She felt hot, weak, scared, nauseas, petrified. She was so frightened that she was frozen and unable to move. She closed her eyes, waiting for the worst, but praying for the best.

Time ticked away. Nothing. Had he not seen her yet? Or was he the type of person that enjoyed messing with people's minds?

She kept her eyes closed and tried to keep her breaths deep and steady.

Corinne continued to wait. And wait. And wait some more.

What was going on? Had he missed her? Did he rob the house and leave already? Was he coming up with some sick plan? What on earth was happening?

She eventually opened her eyes. She cautiously looked up and over. It was still a blur until she turned and faced it completely. It was not a person at all. It was her throw blanket. It hung over the edge of the counter in the hallway leading to the basement.

How on earth did that get there? She hadn't put it there. It hadn't fallen out of the laundry basket because she had just cleaned it a few days ago. One – or maybe both of the cats must have stolen the blanket and dragged it to hallway. Apparently they even tried to jump on the counter with it. Although not typically quitters, it must have been too hard to continue to pull the blanket any further.

Corinne sighed a huge sigh of relief. Her heart began to slow down to a normal pace. The sensation of heat that had washed over her was now dissipating. Moment by moment, she began to feel more human. Once she had truly calmed down, she couldn't help but laugh at the antics of her girls. Leave it to them to keep her on her toes!

"Okay," she said to herself in a breathy voice. "Time to get back to regular life."

"It's right down here," Corinne said as she guided the nice man down the basement stairs.

Corinne waited for the man before turning the corner and showing him the piano. "There it is."

"Oh wow," he replied. He seemed to be a very nice gentleman. A short, somewhat rotund man, probably in his mid-sixties. He had a good head of white, fluffy hair and a small mustache of white and grey rested above his lip. Light blue eyes sparkled through his glasses. Bob was his name, or so Corinne thought he had said. "It is a special piece, but..." He walked over to examine the piano.

"Oh wow! It's an R. S. Howard," he said.

"Are they special or something?"

"Well, you don't see too many of them around." He paused so he could lean in and take a closer look at the piano. "R. S. Howard was based in New York." He continued while also still examining the instrument. "They started making pianos in 1902. The Janssen Piano Company actually built the pianos. Janssen was a bigger manufacturer, and they actually manufactured pianos for several companies, including Howard. Janssen was established in New York City in 1901, and they manufactured the pianos for R. S. Howard until 1932, when they closed due to the Great Depression." Bob explained. "The problem is," he hesitated for a moment. "The condition of your piece. An R. S. Howard that is in good, working condition could fetch you a decent price. This, however..." His voice trailed off.

"I know it's rough," Corinne said. "It came with the house – just like this. I just wanted to see."

Bob's face wrinkled in puzzlement. "How did it get down here? Did you move this all by yourself?"

"No. It was already down here when I moved in. Like I said, this was exactly how I found it."

"Huh." Bob softly grunted. "Well, to be honest, this isn't worth much. I suppose if you wanted to spend the money to fix it up, you could. I just don't know if it would be worth anything. I could look up more information if you like. There are piano restoration companies, too, if you're interested."

"No," Corinne gently responded. "It's not about the money for me. I was just really interested in the history of it. I just wanted to know more about it."

"Okay, I'll tell you what. Let me see if I can find the serial number. If I can, I can at least tell you how old it is." Bob said. He then walked over to the left side of the piano and looked in the corner to get the serial number. He jotted down five numbers that were engraved into a small plaque that rested just to the left of the tuning pins.

"Okay, got it." He said. "Let me look this up and I'll get that information back to you, okay?"

"Oh wow, that's awfully kind of you." Corinne answered. "You don't have to do that."

"It's the least I can do," Bob replied. "Since there's really not much I can do for you here and you had to pay for me to come out, it's the least I can do. I want you to get your money's worth."

"Thank you so much," Corinne said sweetly. "I cannot tell you how much I appreciate it.

"It's no problem. I'll be in touch soon."

Her clothes hung nicely in the closet. They looked so small, though. Her wardrobe didn't even take up half of the closet. It'll be different once Darryl is home. He will gladly use every last inch he can get out of that closet.

Corinne hummed along as she continued to hang up her clothes.

"Chief."

Corinne stopped dead. What was that? Who was that? Who was speaking to her? How could she hear anyone speaking? This was unsettling, to say the least.

All she could do was stand in silence.

Nothing.

Seconds turned into moments turned into minutes.

Still quietness.

What was going on? Who had just spoken?

Corinne heard it. Clear as a bell. Something, or someone, had said the word, 'Chief.' Who was it, though? And why did they say it?

The room was still silent. Even the cats were sleeping, she couldn't even blame this on them.

What was going on? She couldn't hear a thing now, but just a few minutes ago, someone spoke. They spoke to her, or so it seemed. It didn't make sense. Not at all.

Was she seriously losing her mind? Was this isolation becoming too much for her to bear? Did she need to see a therapist? She had never been like this before.

Maybe it was here. Maybe it was Louisville. Was it something here? Was there something in the water? Did this old house have some kind of a gas leak or something that was making her hallucinate? Corinne could not make sense of any of it. She felt as though she truly was losing her mind. Something wasn't right. She didn't know what it was, but something wasn't right.

She took a couple of deep breaths and resumed hanging the last of her clothes. She shook her head continuously trying to make sense of it all.

The phone rang, jerking Corinne out of a nearly asleep state. Her heart pounded in her chest for a few minutes, even after she answered.

"Hello?"

"Hi, is this Corinne Richards?"

"Yes it is."

"This is Bob from Piano Country."

"Oh hi Bob! How are you?"

"I'm good, thanks. I'm calling because I have some information on your piece."

"You do? That's great! Do tell!"

"Well, the piano was built in 1907. So it's well over a hundred years old."

"Wow! That's pretty cool."

"It is! I did a little more digging. I wanted to give you as much information as I could."

"That is so kind of you. Thank you!"

"You're welcome. So, I have an original bill of sale. The Piano was purchased by a woman named Agnes Walker on December

27

fifteenth back in 1907. It was delivered to an address of thirty eight Locust Street."

"That's here. That's my house."

"Interesting. Well I would venture to say then that piano has never left the house. There are no other records of it being sold or moved after that."

"That's odd," Corinne replied.

"Not necessarily. You have to remember that back in those days, a house stayed with the family, and the furniture stayed with the house. So a family member purchases the piano and they leave it with the home. It was as much a part of the home as a fridge or stove or dishwasher would be today. It was functional furniture, if you will."

"Oh, okay. I see what you're saying."

"So, that's all I've got. It's better than nothing."

"It is! That's all really neat! Thank you so much for giving me all of this information!"

"You are very welcome! You have a nice day now."

"You too!"

Corinne ended the call. She hummed to herself. A woman named Agnes Walker purchased that piano and it has been in this house ever since. Very interesting. So the house and the piano share the same history. Corinne desperately wanted to know more of that history.

Chapter Four

Corinne woke to find herself contorted and squished; nearly falling off the bed while the cats rested quite comfortably all spread out over the king size bed. "Figures," Corinne mumbled to herself.

Ugh. Today was the day. The day she had been dreading. Her birthday. Another day older, another day in solitude. Another day in this large, creepy, unfamiliar house. Why couldn't she have a husband with a regular job? Why couldn't she have local friends who would throw her a party? Why did her life have to be like this? Her birthday was nothing more than another anonymous day spent in the vacant house. Oh how she resented this day.

Slowly, regretfully, she rose out of bed. She pulled back the curtain. It was a dismal day. The sky was a horrid charcoal grey color. There were no clouds, simply darkness. Trees bounced back and forth from the potent winds. The rain smacked the Earth harshly. Ick. This day was only getting worse.

With trepidation, Corinne turned on the light switch.

The light came on. Thank goodness she had power! The first - and probably only positive thing about the day.

Corinne moseyed downstairs into the kitchen. She leisurely got herself a cup of coffee. Once her warm brew was ready, she cusped her mug and slowly wandered into the living room. Comfortably curling up on the couch, she pulled a blanket over herself, grabbed her coffee and turned on the television.

No signal.

Oh come on! How could it be that she had electricity, but no cable? Ugh. Doesn't it figure? She hated it. She hated this weather! She hated this house! She hated this day. Everything was just...wrong.

Pianissimo

Corinne lay motionless on the couch. She lay in silence and emptiness. "Happy birthday," she whispered to herself. Some days were just not worth waking up at all.

Corinne decided that today was the day that she would tackle the basement. She needed to get it cleaned up and organized; she hated the cobwebs and chaos down there. It was only a basement, but it still needed to be a more useful space.

She gently shoved the door open with her hip. Carefully managing the stairs, she began to come up with a plan. She would start just beyond the base of the stairs. She'd clear up the cobwebs and dust in the far left corner so that the bins of holiday decorations that sat just beyond the stairs could be put there so she would have more room on the floor.

She held her broom high and began to swing at the cobwebs like a blindfolded child swinging at a piñata. She tried to stand back so that the cobwebs wouldn't fall on her; they flew and swirled all around her – some of them were close, too close. She squeaked and squealed as she swept and swung. The webs had turned into thick yarns, deeply woven into the crevices of the walls. Swipe after swipe somehow created new webs and threads.

After a lengthy battle, it seemed the corner had been finally cleared. Now Corinne faced the daunting task of moving the large, heavy totes. Since they were already stacked, she thought she might just push the towers into the corner. She bent low and pushed with all her might. The totes hardly budged.

"Argh," Corinne grunted. She removed the top box, which was light. She then moved the second tote. That was also fairly light. She finally picked up the bottom tote, which was incredibly heavy. She groaned as she lifted it up. She hurriedly carried it to the corner and put it down.

She took a moment to stretch out her back. After she did, Corinne begrudgingly stacked the other two totes.

Okay. That was done. She had more room at the base of the stairs, and the containers were tucked away in the corner. That was perfect. Time to move onto the next project.

She looked around. There were some cardboard boxes on the floor in the back right hand corner, not far from the piano.

Corinne then decided to go through those boxes. She needed to know what was in them.

She knelt down and began to go through the boxes. Old papers, random pictures and all kinds of miscellaneous items filled the first three boxes. The fourth box was different, though.

The fourth box was in and amongst her belongings, but it didn't seem familiar.

It was actually an old hat box. When or how did they ever get an old hat box? It had to be theirs, right? Why else would it be among her belongings?

She started to sift through the items inside of it. The photos inside were clearly not hers. There were old faded black and white photos of the house and of people from previous generations. As she studied each one, she came across the ancient photo of a woman. The woman's face was vaguely familiar. Corinne looked at the image for several minutes before continuing on. She pulled out the next photo. There was an image that shocked her. The piano, in perfect condition. A woman – that woman. The woman in the previous picture. The woman Corinne had seen her shadowy dream. That tall, elegant older woman who had appeared to her before. She was younger in this image, but her face was exactly the same. Just as in her dream, the tall woman was leaning on the piano. In the photo, she was looking down at another woman. The other woman was seated at the piano, and appeared to be playing. Her gaze, though, was fixated on the taller woman. Corinne flipped the photo over. Agnes and Margaret. December 25, 1907.

This was a family holiday photo. From 1907!

Corinne quickly went back to the previous photo.

Agnes. June 30, 1908.

These pictures had been left for all this time – over a century. And yet, they were in immaculate condition. These women, this house, the piano...it was all amazing and confusing – if not overwhelming – to Corinne. What history had she stumbled upon? Who were these women? What was to be found here?

Hour after hour, Corinne studied the images and relished in the handwriting on the back of each photograph. She dug through the box a little more. She gasped as she grabbed letters, journals, and even more photographs. This was an historic gold mine!

Unable to resist her curious nature, she placed everything back in the box and brought it upstairs. She placed it right next to the couch so she could look at it whenever she wanted.

Corinne woke up on a mission. She was determined to learn the history of the house.

Without any hesitation, she quickly showered, dressed and was out of the door in no time. She had looked up where the town hall was.

Driving carefully into an unknown part of town, Corinne finally found her destination.

She walked in briskly and immediately found the clerk. Well, she was sitting there, but she had her back to the desk.

Corinne grabbed the edge of the counter, almost as if to keep herself from falling. "Excuse me," she said weakly. "I was wondering if I could get the records for my house."

The chair slowly turned around. "What are you looking for?" The clerk was a short, rotund woman with short, curly brown hair. She was hardly looking up at Corinne.

"Everything. I am trying to get the history of the house – any and all information I can get."

The woman rolled her pen up and down the side of her desk. "Oh, I see." She paused. "Did you get an abstract from your lawyer when you purchased your house?"

Corinne waited and thought for a moment. "Yes."

"I recommend going through that again. I mean, I can give you a list based on the town records, but that could cost as much as one hundred dollars for town documents, building permits, residential histories, and such." This woman did not want to be bothered, it seemed. After a moment, she continued. "You should also check the library. They have some great books on local history."

Satisfied with that, Corinne smiled at her. "Okay. Thank you!" She decided to race home to find the abstract.

Once she got home, she ran to the safe and opened it. She pulled out the large folder with all of the mortgage and house's documents in it. She looked through them all.

There! She found it. Corinne pulled it out and began reading.

December 19, 1828: Deed to land of twelve hundred acres. Angus Walker, of New York, to build horse farm on property.

January 20, 1829: Approved permit for construction of one family home, and ten horse barns.

February 16, 1829: Residence completed.

September 8, 1864: Blaze set by rogue confederate soldiers led by Nathen Bedford Forrest destroyed residence, eight horse barns and approximately eight hundred acres of land.

September 30 1864: Construction of a new home and six new barns began.

October 26, 1864: Residence completed.

April 17, 1866: Six hundred acres parceled out and sold to Duane Smith of Louisville.

December 6, 1868: Deed of the house surrendered to Thomas Walker upon the death of Angus Walker.

April 5, 1889: Deed of the house surrendered to Samuel Walker upon the death of Thomas Walker.

July 13, 1905: Deed of the house surrendered to Agnes Walker upon the death of Samuel Walker.

January 8, 1908: Four hundred acres parceled out and sold to William Benson of Louisville.

October 30, 1910: One hundred ninety acres parceled out and sold to Clarke Stevenson of London.

October 17, 1949: House abandoned upon the death of Agnes Walker.

August 16, 1969: House and remaining ten acres sold to Richard "Dick" Mickerson of Louisville.

November 25, 1969: Nine acres parceled out and sold to the town of Louisville.

April 3, 2013: House and remaining one acre sold to Darryl Richards of Las Vegas.

Wow. This house has been through a lot. Over a century of weather, births, deaths, and even a fire! This was getting more interesting by the minute!

The hot water splashed all over the sink as Corinne rinsed off another plate. She placed it on the rack and went to the next one. More soap. She scrubbed the melted cheese off of it. As she scrubbed, Corinne thought she heard something. She paused, only hearing the running water from the faucet.

"Darb."

There it was again. A voice. A strange voice. She couldn't tell if it was a man or a woman speaking. It was almost like a scratchy whisper. It was very weird. It was like nothing she had ever heard before, and yet she couldn't be sure she actually heard anything.

Maybe she hadn't. Maybe it was just her imagination playing games with her. This isolation and solitude was definitely taking a toll on her. It was probably nothing more than that.

She brought her eyes back down to the plate in her hand, and she restarted scrubbing that old, nasty, melted cheese off of it.

The building before her was giant and expansive; it was panoramic. With giant pillars and incredibly intricate stone carvings, this building billowed its own grandness. With both excitement and apprehension, Corinne walked through the giant heavy doors.

Once inside, it was as if she was in an ocean of books. Shelving ran from the floor all the way to the tops of the peaked ceilings. Books of every size, every color. The warm, musty sent of books and antiquity flowed through her nose down into her throat.

She walked over to a desk that was probably as long as her house was wide. There was nothing small about this library.

"May I help you?" A cute rotund woman, probably in her mid-forties asked. She had burgundy retro cat-eye glasses. Her thick hair was pulled back. A light brown shirt rested lightly over her thick frame.

"Yes, hi." Corinne started. "I was wondering if I could get some information on my house. The town clerk said you have some great town history books here."

"Oh yes!" The jovial woman replied. "They are all in the section in the back right corner. Plenty to read."

"Thank you."

Corinne quietly walked over. This section was so full of books. Where should she start? Which ones are the right books? Oh lord. What was she going to do?

She hesitantly paced through the aisle. Back and forth she went, scanning the different book spines. After her third trip down, she finally pulled one down. It sat heavily in her hand. Hopefully this weighted book was weighted with information.

She found a desk, and opened the book. She flipped through the pages until she found the table of contents.

Notable historic homes. Page Ninety two.

Corinne skipped the pages until she came to page ninety two. Her fingers delicately scanned the pages. She looked through picture after picture. Nothing looked right. None of these matched her house. Ugh. Why had she even started on this? What was the point? She was never going to find the information she was looking for.

Suddenly, something caught her eye.

The Walker home. Thirty eight Locust Street, Circa 1846.

That was it! This was what she was looking for! This was her home. Well, sort of. It didn't look anything like it did now. The image showed a grand plantation with endless acres and several large barns. Wow. She never would have recognized it. But that was it. And it was the home of the Walker family, just like the abstract said. She was definitely going to look them up. Corinne figured she now had enough to go on to do research online.

With that in mind, she took the book and made a copy of that page. She folded the page and placed it in her pocket. Corinne then returned the book, thanked the woman and left. She had her mission now.

Corinne lay on the couch, her right leg stretched outright. Her old soccer knee injury was acting up again as a result of all the painting and work she had been doing around the house.

She took some more pain medications and anti-inflammatories to try to ease the pain in her knee. Stupid soccer injury. She remembered how she gave up her piano lessons to play on the soccer team. Just a few games into the season, she hurt her knee and lost both of her passions.

Here she was, years later, just a lonely military wife with no hobbies, passions, no real career of her own. What would have happened if she had continued playing the piano? What would have happened if she hadn't hurt her knee? How different would her life be if things had played out differently? Corinne's mind wandered through the various "what if" scenarios and she quietly drifted off to sleep.

Chapter Five

Corinne clicked on her favorite search engine. In the search bar, she typed "Walker family history and home."

A lengthy list appeared before her. The city's historian website topped the list and seemed to be chock full of information. Corinne clicked on the link.

Angus Walker was a Scottish immigrant. He and his wife, Emma, came to Kentucky after starting a successful horse farm, trade and business in New York. He began the construction of his plantation home in Louisville in 1829.

In 1833, their son, Thomas was born. Two years later, Clarence was born.

With the impending war in the 1860s, Walker quickly found himself in a position to lose everything or gain more than he could imagine. Being a neutral commonwealth, Kentucky was divided and had sympathizers on both sides. Walker decided to use that to his advantage. Selling horses to townsfolk and military elite alike, the Walker family quickly learned of the profits of war.

The horse trade continued to boom; Thomas and Clarence stood to inherit a very profitable business.

Though learning the tact and skill needed to run a booming operation, neither Thomas nor Clarence could stand idly by during the Civil War. They both served in the Confederate army. They enlisted in 1862. Thomas served until 1864, when he was shot in the leg. Clarence never returned from the war.

Before he enlisted, in 1857, Thomas married Nellie Boon. Their twin sons, Jacob and Samuel, were born in 1859. Nellie and Samuel stayed at the plantation with Angus and Emma.

Not long after Thomas' return, the original plantation, eight of the ten original horse barns, several hundred acres went up in flames, twenty horses, and Jacob perished after a Confederate raid led by Nathan Bedford Forrest made its way through the greater Louisville area in 1864.

Not to be kept down, Angus and Thomas Walker built a new home: a smaller, more modest farm house, but still able to accommodate Angus, Emma, Thomas, Nellie and Samuel. After the war, they also sold several parcels of land, decreasing his acreage and their equine population.

Angus Walker lived in the smaller home with Thomas and Nellie until he succumbed to pneumonia in 1868. Emma died later that year.

Thomas continued to run the horse trade, though he was not nearly as successful as his father.

As Thomas and Nellie aged and Samuel became more active in the business, the farm slowly turned into more of a dairy and crop farm than that of a horse farm.

Samuel met and married Mabel Butler, the daughter of a prominent politician.

In 1887, their one and only child, their daughter Agnes, was born.

Samuel, Mabel, and Agnes lived in the village proper until Thomas was no longer to manage the farm.

Samuel and his family returned to the farm in 1889, and Thomas passed at the end of that year. Nellie remained the matriarch of the family until her death in 1892.

Samuel Walker, along with Mabel and Agnes, ran the farm successfully for many years. Samuel and Mabel passed away in 1905 in a tragic accident.

The house remained in Agnes' care until her death in 1949. Being the last in the lineage and being childless, there were no heirs to the farm. Rather, the family estate sat abandoned for two decades.

In 1969, the house was purchased by Dick Mickerson, a successful landlord who owned many properties throughout the greater Louisville region. It was used as a rental property, and finally sold as a private residence in 2013.

Wow! There was a lot of history and a lot of characters connected to this house. This family had seen more than their fair share of tragedies. This was some crazy stuff.

So Agnes Walker was the woman in the pictures. She was the last member of the Walker family, and the one who purchased the piano. Perhaps Corinne needed to start to focus her research onto just Agnes. She figured by doing so, she'd learn about that dilapidated piano downstairs. That was going to be her next mission.

Corinne found herself at the back end of the vacuum once again. Cleaning gave her something to do. She needed to kill time somehow. The whirl of the vacuum was far superior to that of the thunderous silence that normally filled the house.

As she pushed and pulled the large machine, she saw three of her favorite pictures from her wedding on the buffet on the back wall of the dining room. She was cleaning under the watchful eyes of those wedding pictures. She paused and looked at those images.

How different life was on that day. Darryl was present. He looked so handsome in his dress uniform. She was in a princess-like dress. Her hair was perfect. It was a real fairy tale.

Now, here she was with her hair pulled back in a messy pony tail. She donned sweats that were splattered with paint from her other adventures in the house. Darryl was thousands of miles away and most definitely not in his dress uniform. Instead of an overflowing bouquet of perfect flowers, she held a vacuum in her hand. Dear God, how life had changed.

Corinne lost herself in thought and prayed dearly to relive that day again. To have that fairy tale again. To not be vacuuming for the umpteenth time again this week in this horrid, empty house.

Why was the light switch up? Corinne was only just making her way to the basement now. She hadn't turned on the light yet, but the switch was up. Could she have forgotten it and it was on all this time? Since last week?

No, it couldn't be. That was not like her. Besides, the light pooled out from under the door fairly well. She would have noticed if it was on all week.

But, it's on now. And she never touched it. How could that be? This was so bizarre! None of this made any sense. She was certain she hadn't already flipped the switch up, and she was certain she hadn't left it on for the past seven days, either. How did this happen?

Corinne could not make any sense of it at all. It was a very strange mystery. She shook her head, trying to understand what was going on.

With some trepidation, she opened the door and carefully made her way down the stairs carrying the laundry basket.

Everything looked the same. Nothing was out of place, nothing looked unusual. Geez, this was so eerie!

Well, despite whatever it was, everything seemed fine now.

Corinne carried the basket over and began throwing her darks into the washing machine first.

For theirs was a once in a life time love. Corinne closed the book to her predictable romance novel.

She loved romance novels, but she hated them as well. The unrealistic situations and behaviors of the characters, the steamy love scenes – it was all bitter sweet.

As a woman, Corinne loved the idea of these die-hard romances. She pined to have Darryl say cheesy lines like that; she yearned to have the kind of relationship those heroines had. She knew that military wives certainly didn't have that. Neither she nor any of the other women she's met over the years have ever had anything remotely close.

But, she couldn't help but wonder, is that how it is for "normal" people? Do non-military romances play out like that? She envied such people.

Here she was alone, and there was no end in sight. He's been gone for eight months, and he won't be home for another eight. A total of sixteen months. Sixteen months of solitude. Sixteen months from when she had last held her husband. Sixteen months until she can have a steamy romantic evening with him. Sixteen months without hearing his voice or feeling his touch. Sixteen months of nothing.

"No one could possibly understand this kind of isolation and loneliness," she whispered to herself.

Corinne couldn't wait for her search results to come up. Finally!

Here was a link she hadn't seen before. She clicked on it.

On October 11, 1949 Margaret Begum succumbed to Tuberculosis. She was a loving daughter, sister and cousin. She worked as teacher at the primary school. She was a life-long friend of Agnes Walker; they shared a residence until her untimely death. She is survived by her sister, Josephine, and her brother, Walter. Services are to be held on Friday, October 14 at the Episcopalian Church.

Margaret Begum. Corinne wondered who she could be. Life-long friend of Agnes Walker. Hmmm. So she had some connection to the Walker family. She resided in the old farm house. Who on earth could she be? What was her connection to Agnes and the Walker family? Corinne was very curious. She was bound and determined to get answers.

Corinne just sat down. She lit her scented candles and sat down on the couch to relax on a Friday night. Millie and Mollie were curled up sleeping on the far end of the couch. Just as she sat, Corinne saw a dark figure walk past the front door of the living room. She turned quickly, but saw nothing. It was dark out. Perhaps it was just the shadows of the leaves moving in the wind and street lamps. Slightly unsettled, Corinne turned her attention back to the large flat screen TV on the wall in front of her.

Some time had passed and Corinne half-heartedly watched her TV show when she thought she heard something. Ignoring it, she focused completely on the television. She heard the noise again and it crescendoed. She tried to dismiss it, but the sound was relentless. She muted the television. It was then that she heard a man's voice groaning. Corinne jumped up out of fear. She looked around. There was nothing she could grab to protect herself. Corinne jumped backwards onto the couch, grabbed her knees and sat huddled. Then she saw Darryl's old recliner. There was a good hiding spot behind that: between the recliner and the wall. Moving as quickly and quietly as she could, Corinne's feet skipped across the floor and she ducked behind the recliner. Not knowing what else to do, she hoped that she was somehow hiding from this man. As her heart raced, a tear escaped and rolled down her cheek.

Corinne was startled as she watched a dark figure appear, sprint towards the source of the groaning, and then disappear again.

Then there was silence. A loud, haunting, eerie silence. Tears continued to race down Corinne's face.

Slowly and nervously, she stood up. She looked around. Everything seemed the same. The television continued to play on mute.

Corinne tried to slow down her racing heart and inhale deeply. She was still shaken up, though. She returned to her place on the couch. She grabbed Mollie and held her on her lap, hoping to gain some comfort.

"The loneliness is overwhelming. I can feel it in the pit of my stomach. I do things just to do them. There's no meaning to anything. Everything seems empty and pointless. I feel hollow." Corinne heard an echo to her voice, but it wasn't in her phone.

Rachel huffed into the receiver. "Oh Corinne, come on! Stop being so over-dramatic. It's not that bad. Have you called anyone? Have you looked into any of the..."

"No. What's the point?" Corinne grumbled.

"Okay, Eeyore. Call me back when you're done with your pity party." Rachel paused for just a moment before ending the call.

"No one understands." Corinne whispered. Again, she heard that echo.

"Well, based on all of the tests and the exam, I'd have to say your eyes are quite near perfect." Doctor Davis said.

Doctor Davis. Doctor John Davis, to be exact. He had the best reviews on-line of any of the local ophthalmologists. Corinne had instilled so much hope and certain expectations into today's appointments, and he was not saying what she wanted him to.

"Are you sure? There must at least be some kind of age changes or something. Macular degeneration, maybe?"

He shook his head. "Nope. Not at all. Your eyes look incredibly healthy. Your vision is exactly where it should be for a person of your age. You're too young for any significant vision changes yet."

"There's got to be something." She pleaded.

"No, I really don't see anything wrong or unusual with your eyes."

"Maybe you're missing something, then. What other tests can you run?"

He sat back in his chair. "Okay. Why don't you tell me what's going on. You're quite insistent that there is something wrong. What are you seeing or experiencing that makes you so sure there's a problem?"

"Nothing. Everything. It's weird."

"Do you care to elaborate?"

"It's just – I don't even know where to begin. I..." She tried to calm her thoughts. "I see shadows. Any time. Day or night. There might not even be anything there. Sometimes they move. It's just bizarre." She hesitated. "I...see things that aren't there. Things don't look like they should. It's just not right. I've never had vision problems before. I've never had anything like this. There has to be something wrong with my eyes!"

The doctor shifted in his chair. "Miss Richards, I see nothing wrong with your eyes. They are quite strong and healthy – as they should be for a woman of your age. If you're really concerned about seeing apparitions and such, I highly recommend that you call another kind of doctor."

He stood up and walked out of the exam room. The strong bang of the door closing made Corinne jump. She was shocked at his demeanor. He had seemed so pleasant at first. But clearly he wasn't. How rude!

Sucking up her wounded pride, Corinne stood up, took a couple of deep breaths and left the office. She was going to figure out what was going on one way or another.

Chapter Six

Corinne stared at the piano. Was she really going to do this? Did she even know what she was doing? No. No, she wasn't completely sure.

Really? Who was she kidding? She had never done anything like this. She had never taken shop class in school. Her father and brothers would never let her help or teach her anything handy.

"Stick with girly stuff!" Her brother Ryan always said.

She and her mom were outnumbered. Dad and three boys. The four of them were like their own little exclusive club. Corinne was never allowed to do anything with them.

Her brothers always picked on her. That's what big brothers were for, right? Wasn't it normal for them to tease and make fun of her?

She remembered how when she hurt her knee in soccer, Tom told her she should have just stayed with girlie things like playing the piano.

He was right. Look at her now. Back at a piano, but with a different mission. Could she really do this, though? She didn't know what she was doing. She's never done anything like this - not even close! It wasn't like there was anyone around to show her or teach her.

Forget it. There was no reason to do this. It was pointless. She'd only make things worse. Stupid idea. What was she thinking?

She shook her head at herself and walked back upstairs.

Agnes Walker. Corinne waited for the search results. Hardly anything came up.

Corinne scrolled through the few items. Here was something: Remembering the Walker Legacy.

Pianissimo

Miss Agnes Walker of thirty eight Locust Street is an educator at the primary school in Louisville. She has been teaching there for a number of years.

She is the last descendant of Angus Walker, a Scottish Immigrant who came to Louisville from New York in 1829.

At this year's Louisville Fair, we will be honoring great members of Louisville past and present. Miss Walker will be featured in the parade to honor her family and their Louisville legacy.

That was pretty cool. That must have been a great experience for Agnes to honor the entire family.

It was so weird to think that such a predominant, powerful family once lived in the same house that Corinne lives in now. Kind of weird, but kind of cool. She lived in a house where famous people once lived.

"Oh yes. We live in the Walker home." Corinne put on a silly, haughty voice. "No, it sounds better," she corrected herself. "We live in the Walker estate. Oh yes that sounds much better! We live in the Walker estate." She laughed at herself.

The cats looked up at her.

"Oh hello, ladies. How kind of you to join me for high tea at the Walker estate." She did a small, silly, little 'fancy' dance in her chair.

The cats continued to look at her with puzzlement in their feline eyes.

Corinne laughed. Maybe she's lost her mind. Maybe. Hey, at least she's having fun for a change.

The dim light barely lit the old dilapidated instrument. Corinne stared at it.

What was she going to do with it? Just let it rot as it has been for however long? She couldn't sell it. No one in their right mind would purchase something in such horrid condition. She couldn't fix it.

Well, maybe she could. She didn't really know how to, though. The boys always told her to leave the typically masculine jobs to them. She was just a stupid girl.

46

Well, she wasn't that stupid, was she? No. She had some good points. She knew how to do some stuff. Just not this. But she could learn, couldn't she? Maybe look some stuff up on the internet? She could. She could just try, right? Why not?

Screw what the boys said! They were just being obnoxious. They didn't know how good she really was at all kinds of things, including soccer and music. It was hard to ignore the old insults she had been holding onto all of these years. They had taken up permanent residence in her mind.

But you know what? She wasn't doing this to win any kind of competition. She wasn't doing this so she could sell it. She was doing it just to see. It was in such crappy shape, even if she made it worse, who would care? It wouldn't make a difference. Anything had to be better than this, right? Hopefully. She'd either come out on top or at least come out of this learning some things on how to be handy. It was a win-win situation.

She breathed deeply. She grabbed the sandpaper and stepped closer to the piano.

"You can't do this. You'll ruin it no matter what you do," she heard in her head.

"No! It's already ruined. I'm trying to help it. I'm trying to fix it. Everybody has to start somewhere. The only way I can learn is if I do this on my own!" She said out loud. "Alright, here it goes."

Corinne started at one side on the piano. The side paneling had the most amount of wood and wouldn't be as tricky or intricate as the face. She sorted through until she found the right size: sixty.

She placed the paper to the panel and started pushing. With all of her might, she began sanding the piano. Up and down and up and down and up and down. She leaned in, pushing harder. Beads of sweat immediately formed and sped down her face. She pushed more and more. Her elbows were beginning to hurt. She stopped and pulled the sandpaper away. It was thinner...maybe. It seemed like it might be a little better. Apparently, this paint was on thick.

"Holy crow!" She sighed. She should have gotten paint thinner. But she really didn't want to use that noxious stuff – especially in the basement with no ventilation. If she could only get that small amount done with that much effort, she was in for one very long restoration. This tiny bit took a tremendous amount of elbow grease. Should she get a sander? Maybe. She had no idea on how to use it, though. She'd never used any kind of power tool before. Maybe they could teach her in the hardware store. She could only hope.

For now, though, all she had was herself. And you know what? She was going to push through! She wasn't going to let that nasty green paint win. No, she was going to bust her behind and get this thing done. It may take her a while, but she was determined to restore this old instrument back to its original, beautiful condition. This was going to be her project and she was going to succeed!

Taking in a nice, deep breath, Corinne placed the sand paper against the side of the piano again and she began pushing it with all her might. Little tiny green particles flew all around her. It didn't long before she was covered in them. That was okay, though. It meant she was making progress.

She continued on and on for hours. She'd occasionally stop and give her arms a rest. Each time she did, she could see that some of the original Mahogany wood was beginning to appear. Finally! There was some light! The wood was still alive underneath that awful paint job! She was feeling excitement, pride and accomplishment. The boys were wrong. She could do this and she did do this successfully. This project may be long and difficult, but it was definitely going to be worth it!

The outside world was morphed and swirled around through the old leaded glass. Corinne stole an extra glance at the warped view as she vacuumed the cat hair off the area rug and then the couch. She smiled at the quirkiness of the old windows. Sweat raced down her face as she cleaned diligently despite the horrid hot, humid weather. After several minutes, she finally stopped the vacuum.

As soon as the whirl of the motor died down, Corinne thought she heard something. She strained to hear it. After concentrating for a few silent moments, she could finally make out the faint sound of a woman crying.

Why was there a woman crying? Was someone hurt? Did something happen? Corinne hoped whoever it was was alright.

Panic stricken for the other person, Corinne ran through the house looking in every room, opening every door. What was going on? Who was that? There was no one in the house. She ran out through the back door to see if any of her neighbors were hurt. Not one sign of life. What in the world? Something had to be happening. She could still hear the cries.

Corinne walked briskly back into the house. As she came in, she felt drawn to the inside basement door. Corinne went to slide back the lock, but it was so hot, it singed her hand. Corinne immediately removed her hand from the door. She looked at her palm which was blazing red. She blew gently on it to try to ease the scorch. The crying was clearer now.

Braving the lock once again, Corinne quickly undid the latch. She pushed the door open with all her might. The darkness rose up the stairs like billowing clouds of smoke. There it was. The crying was clear and loud now. A woman wept down in dark, dank basement.

"Hello?" Corinne's voice trembled with fear. "Hello? Who are you? Are you ok? Do you need help?"

Her voice echoed mildly down the stairs.

The crying continued.

"Who are you? Are you okay? Do you need help?" Corinne repeated herself.

Still no response, only sobs.

Corinne stood at the stop of the stairs, frozen with fear. The burn on her hand began to throb. She looked at her hand. Her palm was red and beginning to blister. Yet, there were no signs of fire. No smoke, there was no scent of anything burning, no crackling or visible flames. Was it possible the fire had only just begun? Why was the door so hot that she couldn't touch it? If she were to go down there to help this woman, would she end up hurt herself? She was truly torn: unsure of whether to brave the basement stairs or tend to her hand.

After a perceived eternity, the sobbing suddenly began to fade away. Just as when it began, Corinne found herself straining to hear this woman once again. Eventually, there was utter silence.

Now paralyzed by both fear and confusion, Corinne stood in place and looked back at her hand. The blister was gone and her palm looked completely normal. No longer red, no longer painful. As if nothing had happened, life in the house was still and peaceful again.

Chapter Seven

Corinne hurriedly dialed the number. "C'mon! C'mon, pick up the phone!" She quietly said while the other end rang.

The answer machine started to speak. There was a screech. Finally! Her voice. "Hello?"

"Rachel?!" Corinne said, frightened.

"Yeah. What's up Corinne? Are you okay?"

"I...don't know." She said with great panic.

"Honey, what's wrong? Do you need help?"

"I..." Corinne struggled to breathe. "I think there are...ghosts here."

Rachel was silent.

"Rachel?" Corinne shouted into the receiver.

There was a long pause before Rachel spoke up. "Seriously?"

"There are ghosts here! This house is haunted!"

Again, silence.

"I'm serious! There's something in this house!"

Rachel sighed heavily into the phone. "Okay, you think your house is haunted."

"I know it is!"

"And you want me to do what about it?" Rachel clearly did not understand. There was no sympathy.

"Forget it!" Corinne began to cry.

"Corinne," Rachel back-paddled. "I'm worried about you. The longer you're in that house alone..." She stopped herself. "Are you okay?"

Corinne's voice cracked. "Yeah. I think so."

"So, what makes you think there are ghosts in the house?"

"I can see them, and hear them, and sometimes even feel them."

"Wow! Okay. So, you believe in ghosts?"

"I...I don't know. I never really thought about it before."

"But now you do?"

"Well, yeah. I...guess."

"You guess?"

"I know what I've seen and heard and felt and experienced!"

"Well, that's good. Right?"

"Listen, don't treat me like I'm crazy!"

"I won't! I'm not!" Rachel defended herself. She took a couple of deep breaths that Corinne could hear. "Why don't you tell me what's going on. What have you seen?"

"I..." Corinne struggled to breathe. "I've seen things. Like shadows and people. Things move. Like this one day, there was a wire hanging over a nail that hadn't been there before. And one time the light switch for the basement was on before I ever came down to turn it on."

"Wow. That's kinda weird." Rachel responded.

"And then, just this morning..." The tears began to flow heavily. "There was crying. I could hear someone crying in the basement. And when I went to grab the door knob, I burnt my hand – like there was a fire down there. But there wasn't! It was hot and dark and a woman was crying, and then all of a sudden it all just stopped. And my hand wasn't burnt anymore."

"Are you serious?"

"Absolutely! This just happened. And I'm all alone and scared and there's no one here to help me!" Corinne paused. "I went and got my eyes checked and they're fine. There's nothing wrong with my sight. My eyes are completely normal. Everything is completely normal, except for this house."

"So what are you going to do?"

"I don't know. What am I supposed to do?"

"Maybe...call a priest and get an exorcism or something."

Corinne stopped and contemplated what Rachel had just said. "Yeah, I guess I could do that."

"Corinne, I'm really worried about you. This move has been really bad for you. You've completely isolated yourself. You've never reached out to other military wives. You're not acting the way you normally do. And now this. Something's gotta give. Either you move out of there, or try to make some friends or do something. This isn't right. It's not healthy, and it's definitely not normal."

Corinne sobbed. Rachel was right...to some extent. But she couldn't just up and move. They bought this house! She had no desire to go out and meet new people. She was lonely, but she was lonely for Darryl. She couldn't give a hoot about anyone else.

Was Rachel right? Or was she just being insensitive? She clearly didn't believe in this. It didn't seem that she really cared at all. Corinne couldn't figure things out. She needed some quiet time. She needed to sit down and think about who she was and what she wanted out of life, out of her marriage, out of her friendships, even out of this house.

"Okay. Yeah. Thanks," she feebly responded before hanging up. This was not at all what she had expected.

Dust and small particles of paint swirled in the air around her. Corinne kept pushing, harder and harder. She paused to wipe the sweat off her forehead. The paint was nearly gone. She looked down at the sandpaper in her hand. It was fairly well used, but she might be able to finish it all without getting a new one.

She reached for the top right corner of the side panel again. With as much strength as she could muster, she slid the sandpaper up and down and up and down. Her elbows were aching. She pushed harder. The scratching of the sandpaper against the wood was rhythmic. She pushed and pushed. The last paint chip eventually disappeared.

Corinne reached for her bottle of water and chugged it down quickly.

She just had that last little piece on the bottom left corner. The problem was the decorative molding. It was raised just enough that trying to get the pain off in that corner was a challenge. She slowly knelt down. What if she...No. That wouldn't work. Hmmm. Maybe...no. That wasn't feasible either.

She folded the sandpaper into a tight triangle over her index finger. Using that, she came in at a ninety degree angle and began pushing the sandpaper up and down in small, but powerful movements. She was able to get in right along the border of the molding. She scratched and scratched and scratched. She went over the molding as well. She pushed and pulled the sandpaper as quickly as she could. After a couple of minutes, she let it go and looked at the piano.

There. It was gone. The old mahogany wood was showing. She read that she was going to need to use fine grit sandpaper now just to help clean it up and make it soft and smooth. But the first side was done. It looked pretty good, too.

This was by no means an easy task, but Corinne relished in a great sense of accomplishment. This was more fun than she had expected.

She finished the last of her water. She couldn't do any more. She was pretty much wiped out from all this. But that was okay. She had no deadlines. She could work with the fine sandpaper another time. Or perhaps, she'd wait until she was able to get all of the paint off of the entire upright piano. She'd figure it out. One way or another, she was going to revitalize this old instrument.

Corinne lay in bed with the television quietly playing as her final distraction before sleep. Millie and Mollie were happily contorted on the bed, dreaming little kitty dreams. As Corinne watched the predictable sitcom, her mind happily faded into nothingness. No need to think or feel; she was focused solely on the small screen not too far from the end of her bed.

Some time had passed and Corinne found herself beginning to slip into the early stages of sleep. Slam! There was a sudden, loud noise coming from downstairs – it sounded like a door had closed – more as if it was slammed shut with tremendous power. It was so loud and so hard, she could feel the reverberations. She felt the bed shake. The whole room had shook! It felt as though even the floor and walls had trembled.

She immediately shot up in bed, looking around. What had just happened? Nothing was out of place in the bedroom. She looked over and saw the girls were still sleeping in their unusual positions. She feared going downstairs: what if someone had just broken into her house? She was defenseless. If she stayed up here and remained quiet, might she have a better chance of surviving? The house was quiet, though. She couldn't hear anyone or anything.

Corinne muted the television. Nothing. Not one sound emanated from the first floor. Nothing was being moved nor was anything broken. No footsteps could be heard. She slowly slid herself out from under the covers and looked out the window and peered down at the driveway below. No unusual cars. From what she could see, the backdoor seemed to be intact.

She cautiously slipped back in to her bed. Looking around, she felt as if she was losing her mind. She knew she had heard that door shut. She felt the vibrations! And yet, nothing indicated that anything had happened. Even the cats still slumbered. This did not make any sense.

It was going to be a weird, long, sleepless night for Corinne.

On the second shelf was something that looked promising. Oh wait. No. It's a grinder, not a sander. Hmm. She looked at the shelf below it.

"Can I help you?" The salesman ducked down to look Corinne in the eye.

"Oh! Hi." She said weakly.

"Is there anything I can help you with?"

"Maybe. I'm looking for a sander."

"Okay. What are you looking to do? What are you sanding? Is it flooring? A deck?"

"No. A piano."

The man looked very confused. "A piano?"

"Yeah. You see, there's this very old piano in the basement and I want to fix it. It's been painted, so I'm trying to get all the paint off."

"Why do you have a painted piano in your basement?"

Corinne shook her head. "I don't know. It was like that." She paused briefly. "I just moved in."

"Oh, okay." He waited for a second. "So, you probably have a lot of detail work, I would assume."

"Yes. But there's also big flat pieces. I've been doing it all by hand, but if I could use something like a sander, that would make it so much easier!"

"Yeah it would!" He motioned for her to follow him. "Come with me."

They walked a few feet and stood before several different sanders. "So, these are probably going to be your best bet. They are less expensive as they aren't for real heavy duty work. But, they aren't too cheap that they'd fall apart on you or anything."

"Okay," Corinne hesitantly replied. "What's the easiest to use?"

He walked over to a small, blue, round sander. He placed his hand on top of it. "This one. It's an orbital sander. The bottom is like Velcro, so you can just place the sand paper right on it and go."

"Okay. I like that. That sounds easy enough. So, yeah, I'll take one."

He reached the shelf under the display and pulled out a box. "Great! Now, for the detail work, you're probably going to want to use a Dremmel or something."

Corinne shifted her weight and pressed her lips together. "You know, I'm not really sure I want to get one. I almost kind of think I'd like to do the detail stuff by hand."

The salesman's eyes grew wide, and his eyebrows rose. "Are you sure? Do you understand how difficult and tedious that will be?"

"I do. I know I sound crazy, but I just feel like there is something to be said for the satisfaction of doing it by hand."

The man's face was very twisted in confusion.

"If I don't like it or it's too much, I can always come back and buy one, right?"

He inhaled deeply. "I guess so." He paused for several moments. "So, you're all set then?"

Corinne smiled and nodded. "Yeah, I am. Thanks!"

He handed her the box, and she gleefully walked over to the checkout line.

Chapter Eight

Corinne brought a small load of laundry down the rickety stairs into the basement. Humming a random melody to herself, she casually walked into the somewhat dank cellar, when something caught her eye. A figure stood by the old mangled piano. It was her – the woman from her dream and in those pictures! It was Agnes! Tall and lean, and figure and her face were undeniable. How could she see Agnes? Agnes lived here over a century ago! This was really weird. Was she really looking at Agnes, or was her mind playing more tricks on her?

Slowly, Agnes turned to look at Corinne. Her face was wrinkled, yet regal. Her hair was elegantly worn up. Her clothes were an echo of days gone by. Her eyes grew wide and bright for a moment. "Margaret?" There was an unusual quality to her voice. A whisper, and yet a scream; clear, yet scratchy. Hers was a voice like none Corinne had ever heard before.

Corinne stood, holding the laundry basket, unable to move.

"Margaret?" Agnes spoke again. She seemed to look directly at Corinne, if not through her.

Corinne was completely powerless to speak.

She watched Corinne for several moments. Then, the excitement quickly diminished from her eyes. "Margaret." Her voice quailed. Tears began to slide down her high cheek bones. "Margaret," she gently cried again.

Corinne blinked. When her eyes reopened, Agnes was gone and Corinne found herself in a strange solitude.

A heavily decorated Christmas tree stood in the background. An older man and woman stood in the middle. He had thick white hair. His face was well worn and wrinkled. A grey suit hung loosely on his thin, hunched frame. She wore her hair in a perfect bun. A prim and proper white blouse flowed beautifully over her arms and torso. A long grey skirt surrounded her legs and swept the floor.

On the other side of her stood a younger woman. Her curly hair was mostly up, but some loose curls danced around her face. Her clothes mimicked the clothes of the older woman. The younger woman held what looked to be a small child. She wore a little white dress. White stockings covered her tiny legs. And she wore miniscule black shoes.

On the outer side of the older gentleman was a younger man. He bore a strong resemblance to the older man. His thick hair was dark, though. He boasted a large, thick moustache as well. His dark suit was dashing. This was a handsome family.

Corinne flipped the picture over. Thomas, Nellie, Samuel, Mabel and baby Agnes. Christmas 1889.

This was so surreal. Here they are. People. Real people. They're not just names. Now she knew their faces. This was the Walker family. The Walker family. It was crazy to think that these people once lived in the house she now calls home. And this was the last time they would ever be seen as a complete family. Thomas died right after Christmas. This was incredible. There was so much importance and greatness to this one little photograph. What a find!

How sad that the family was gone, though. That there was no one to take over this house. Corinne couldn't give these pictures to anyone, to treasure these family heirlooms. Perhaps she should take them on as her own heirlooms. Someone needed to treasure these pictures and belongings, why not her?

The Walker family was now Corinne's family.

July 18, 1969 - At the town hall meeting last week, the subject of the old Walker farm homestead and property was brought up for discussion.

Neighbors of the property expressed their concerns and discontent with condition of the dilapidated house and unkempt property. Siting that it was a source of entertainment for local hoodlums and juvenile delinquents, the neighbors all propositioned the village to take over the care of the property.

Agnes Walker died in 1949. She was the last in the Walker lineage, leaving no one behind to reside in or care for the property. The house has been sitting abandoned ever since.

After a lengthy discussion as to whether or not the home could be restored under the city's historic restoration grant, local business man Dick Mickerson offered to take over the care and restoration of the property, if the village would allow. Pending research on the proper protocol since there was no current deed to the house, the village agreed to terms with Mr. Mickerson. A closing date of mid-August is projected. Mickerson plans on restoring the old building and offering it as off-campus housing for University of Louisville students.

The piano was back in its original state; the wood was slightly dulled from time, but still beautiful. A young man looked at it intently.

"It's a beautiful piece – it's a shame, but we don't have any other choice."

Suddenly, there was a large mob all crowded into the small room. A giant unending staircase lay before the piano. The group began to all laugh and cheer.

Millie and Mollie came into the room, and somehow together, the two cats became one large toucan. The toucan perched on top of the piano.

The laughter grew louder.

"One! Two! Three!" They all shouted.

The piano was pushed down the staircase. The toucan laughed and pecked at the piano as a woodpecker would.

A butcher then appeared and began to chop large slabs of meat on the top of the piano while the toucan still pecked away.

The piano sped down further and further, and yet it always seemed as the crowd was right there rolling in laughter.

A large cascade of water came down and doused the piano. The butcher continued to cut, and the toucan continued to peck.

The laughter crescendoed and crescendoed and crescendoed.

Pianissimo

Beep. Beep. Beep. The beeping continued and went on incessantly.

Finally, Corinne rolled over and slowly opened her eyes. The alarm clock was doing its job – far too well. Corinne finally slapped the top of the clock to silence it – at least for now.

She lay in bed. She didn't want to open her eyes, but she was not falling back asleep, either.

What a weird dream! What did any of it mean? Why on earth was there a mob? Who was the butcher? How did her two cats turn into a toucan? Why on earth was she even dreaming of the old piano anyway?

Yes, it was old and beat up. But really? This was just stupid. This is the best her imagination could come up with?

Corinne chuckled at herself. That was so weird; so, so weird. Oh well.

She shook off the dream and got up to face another day.

Corinne's hands lightly caressed the keys as she walked past the piano. The urge to play quickly consumed her. Unable to resist, she stopped in place. As if she were possessed, her right hand began to create a song that had long been buried deep in Corinne's memory. She wasn't consciously pressing the keys, her hand was working of its own accord.

A melody was actually coming out of the old, ugly piano. The music itself was anything but old or ugly. Corinne played along and then pressed a key that didn't sound quite right. It wasn't that the piano was out of tune, the note just didn't sound right.

Maybe it was the wrong note. Which key would it be, then?

G. It came to her. It was almost as if it had been whispered to her. How strange it is that our thoughts sometimes seem like conversations – as if she truly had heard a whisper.

Corinne turned to better face the piano. She placed both hands on the old, worn keys. Unexpectedly, she felt a light, cold pressure over her hands. She closed her eyes and inhaled deeply.

With one more deep breath, Corinne began to play. What had only been a simply melody moments ago, was now a song – a real song. There was a melody and a harmony. Notes were exquisitely escaping the old piano. The song came out of Corinne – and the piano effortlessly. Corinne lost herself in the music.

Millie and Mollie raced around the house, nearly tripping Corinne as she came down the stairs. Corinne smiled as she watched the girls race and play. Cat toys were scattered about and she could hear something jingling and rolling around. Corinne peered around the corner. The girls were playing with their toys. Suddenly, they leapt up and ran through the kitchen, dining room and into the living room. They jumped on and off the couch. The girls unexpectedly interrupted their play and both looked up. Corinne looked to see what they were looking at, but saw nothing. Both cats began reaching up and swatting at what seemed to be nothing more than thin air. They continued to do so and seemed quite engaged in play. All Corinne could do was watch in joyful curiosity. She had no idea what they could possibly be playing with, but they were definitely enjoying themselves. Perhaps a small bug? Some random bit of dust? Whatever it was, it had their full attention.

The cats' play went on for several minutes. Corinne's mind drifted off and she had lost track of time. It was a nice reprieve to not think about things, but just get lost in the innocent play of the cats.

Quiet laughter was soon heard in the background. It wasn't an evil laugh, it was a genuinely happy, sweet laugh.

Corinne looked around. There was no one there. Who was laughing? Was it her? Had she gone that crazy that she didn't even know that she was laughing at the cats' antics? That had to be it. The cats were highly entertaining. But boy did she need to get out!

Chapter Nine

Seven. Corinne wrote the number seven in her Sudoku puzzle. She was sprawled out on the couch. Millie was sleeping on her legs, Mollie was curled up between her and the back cushions. It was a nice, quiet, peaceful, relaxing morning.

Corinne's eyelids were just starting to get a little heavy. Maybe she'd allow herself a late morning nap.

Just as she placed the Sudoku book down on her chest, she heard someone say, "Bless you." It was loud, but it was a whisper. It was enough of a whisper that she couldn't figure out if the voice was masculine or feminine; and it was loud enough for her to hear – and it sounded as though it came all the way from the back of the house.

Corinne just laid there. She knew no one else was in the house. Was she starting to dream? She was tired, but she wasn't that tired.

It was just like those other times where she's heard people speak. It's clear as a bell. There's no question that she hears these things. It was odd, no doubt about that. It was a gentle voice; it really wasn't scary. In some bizarre way, Corinne wasn't too disturbed by it.

Whether she was losing her mind, or the house was haunted, it didn't really matter. There was nothing she could do about either of them. So she just let it go.

Still feeling peaceful, she decided to close her eyes and take a little nap.

Corinne gently and carefully placed the handful of photos into the small bag. She sealed it closed. These were the images she had seen. She figured that as she went through the box, she would place pictures and any letters or documents into plastic zipper bags so she knew she what she had already viewed, and she was helping to preserve them.

She grabbed another handful of photographs and spread them out the floor in front of her. She reached into the box and found an envelope overflowing with papers. She decided to look at those first.

My Dearest Mabel,

How lonely it is to be on this rail tour and not be in your presence. My heart is not with me; it has taken root in Louisville and remains with you at all times.

The scenery is quite lovely as we pass by. Lush green fields, large ancient trees. We should be coming up to the mountains very soon.

Mother and Father are greatly enjoying themselves on this adventure. It is a delight to see them so jovial and excited despite their age. I am actually quite impressed that they even decided to venture out like this. At their age, most people are somewhat reclusive. Or at least not out very far or for very long spans of time.

We have just been alerted that it is time for luncheon. So I'd best end this here.

Please know that I love and miss you with every fiber of my being.

Samuel.

Corinne smiled. What a cute, sweet little love note from days gone by. This letter was far too cute. Corinne gently folded it up and placed it in the bag.

She reached into the envelope and pulled out another paper.

July 5, 1905 – Mr. Samuel Walker, and his wife, Mabel, passed last evening after a tragic accident.

The couple was driving to their home when fireworks had been sent off closely to the road as the couple's carriage passed by. Their horse became frightened, it began to run and swerve manically, on-lookers say.

Judd Winslow attempted to jump into the street, and grab the reins with the hopes of calming the horse and saving the Walkers. Unfortunately, as Mr. Winslow approached the carriage, the horse reared. The carriage fell backwards, the horse quickly followed, crushing them. According to doctors, they most likely passed right away due to the severity of the accident.

They are survived by their only child, Agnes. Services are to be held this Saturday, July 8, and Sunday, July 9.

Wow! Agnes became an orphan at the age of eighteen. What a horrible way to lose her parents! She was left all alone to somehow manage a farm by herself. This was tragic. Corinne felt pity for Agnes; hers was not an easy life. You would think that a girl coming from such a prestigious family would have everything handed to her on a silver platter. That, sadly, was not the case for poor Agnes.

Corinne gently folded the newspaper clipping back up and gently placed it in the bag. She slowly rose to her feet. After reading that horrible story, she needed a break from all this. Maybe she'd go get a cold drink from the refrigerator.

The whirl of the sander and the grinding of sandpaper against wood was all Corinne could hear. She wiped the sweat and debris from her face. This side was nearly done. This was such a long process. The paint was on so thick it was ridiculous. Who would paint a piano anyway? And not even a nice color. It was a drab, olive green. Darryl's fatigues looked better than this! She was enjoying the work, but she could not get past the idea of someone painting a piano.

She shook her head and resumed her sanding. The sander began shaking and vibrating in her hands. She placed it back on the wood of the piano and she sanded away. She pushed and guided it until every little last speck of green was gone.

She stopped the sander again, and took the paper off. Where was that medium grit paper? She looked around the dim basement until she saw it on the floor, right behind her. She bent down, grabbed one and placed it on the sander.

Once again, it whirled and buzzed. She pushed it back and forth again. She went all the way to the edges. She went all over. She sanded and sanded and sanded some more. She sanded this part of the piano until the sheet of medium grit was completely used up.

She looked on the floor and found her fine grit paper. She grabbed one of those and put it on the sander.

Pianissimo

She started up the sander and repeated the process again. Up, down, and all around she sanded. She went back and forth going over every little spot numerous times. She sanded as much as she could, until her hands and elbows began to ache from all of this hard work.

After she turned the machine off, she ran her hands on the piano. The wood was so smooth and soft. It felt light and gentle. She never knew wood could feel this way. It was as silky as wood could feel. She could not get over how smooth it was. She really liked how this felt. Maybe she should go into woodworking.

Corinne laughed at herself. Not likely. But regardless, she was enjoying every moment of this restoration project; she absolutely loved the finished product.

Samuel was a short man. Shorter than Corinne had expected. He was hardly three inches taller than Mabel. His wedding picture with her was stereotypical, Corinne thought. They both stood extremely upright. The both wore serious expressions on their faces. Her dress was a long, lacey one. Simple, but pretty in its own right. His suit was a dark grey suit. The sleeves looked a bit too short for his long, gangly arms. They were cute...sort of. This photo was more iconic than it was joyful.

Corinne scooped it up by the corner and gently dropped it into the bag. She smiled. Her bags were becoming increasingly full. She was having fun going through all these old things.

She looked over at the clock. 3:14. Geez! She wasted a huge part of the day just looking at photos. She'd better get up and start doing something! She couldn't let this day be a complete waste!

The refrigerator door closed with a loud thump. Groceries were finally all put away. And just in the nick of time!

Rain started gushing down from the sky. It was coming down hard and it was coming down fast. It was hitting the leaves with such force that it sounded as if she were surrounded by a large waterfall.

She opened the windows so she could better hear the rush. She inhaled that light, sweetly scented rain air. This was nice. This was peaceful. This was serene.

This was the perfect weather to curl up under a blanket, drink some tea, and read a book. Corinne loved days like that. They were just perfect.

Here she was being given an opportunity for a perfect afternoon. Corinne thought for a moment. Maybe she'd give herself the rest of the day off so she could enjoy this perfect afternoon.

She got some water boiling, and she ran upstairs to get her book.

When she came back, the tea kettle was whistling. She poured the hot water into a mug with a tea bag in it. She grabbed the cup, she grabbed her book and curled up on the couch. This was going to be a nice, relaxing afternoon.

Baby Agnes 1887. She looked like a little doll. She wore a classic white dress. It enveloped her: it was quite large. Her little head peeked out from the top of the dress. She had wispy, dark baby hair. She was propped up in a large chair.

Corinne chuckled looking at Agnes' little baby facial expression. It was just too cute, and it was very funny.

Kids nowadays wouldn't sit for a picture like this. They can hardly sit for a few seconds, let alone for the lengthy process taking a picture was back then.

Little Agnes just sat there, liked a propped up puppet. What a great image!

Neither Samuel nor Mabel was in the picture. Just Agnes. A tiny, little Agnes. A precious, baby Agnes. Even more than a century old, she was still an adorable baby.

It was eight o'clock on a Saturday night. There was nothing good on television. So Corinne just used it as background noise. With nothing better to do, she reached into the envelope and pulled out a newspaper clipping.

The Louisville School District is proud to welcome Miss Agnes Walker to their teaching faculty.

Miss Walker is only child of Samuel and Mabel Walker, the last in the great Walker lineage.

Pianissimo

Miss Walker is a native of Louisville and resides in her family's home just outside of the town proper.

When she is not teaching, Miss Walker enjoys spending time with her horse, Chief; she crochets, and she occasionally takes in injured little baby birds and rabbits and nurses them back to health.

She has experience and knowledge in history, literature, and science. Miss Walker shall be teaching at the primary school starting this autumn.

Huh. That was interesting. She was like a little wildlife veterinarian – a 'Doctor Do-little' in her own right. Corinne got a small chuckle out of that.

She sifted through more pictures. She began to lay them all out on the coffee table. She reached back into the box while staring at one of the photographs. Her hand hit something hard. What was that? Corinne finally looked down into the box.

It was a book! She clutched it and brought it up onto the table. She carefully opened the front cover.

Agnes Walker 1907.

With gentle trepidation, Corinne turned the first page.

Dear Diary,

Thus another school year returns. I have quite a large class this year with twelve students. I certainly do hope they won't be too trying.

There's a new teacher with us this year. Her name is Margaret Begum. She's a lovely lass. From Louisville, but she worked at another school elsewhere prior to now. She's quite a handsome lady, and a delight to talk to. I do believe I have found myself a new friend in her.

Eleanor and Hattie have been pressuring me a bit to find a good suitor. As I am about to turn twenty years, it is high time I was at least seeing someone, or so they tell me. The trouble is, I don't fancy anyone. I have encountered plenty of men in my life, but none have ever truly grabbed my attention. Truth be told, I much prefer the company of women! Hattie would have an absolute fit were she to hear me say that. I suppose I don't see what all the fuss is about. As an only child on a farm, I've always been a self-sufficient woman. I see no wrong in tending to the necessities of the house as a man might. For Heaven's sake, it is much easier now as the farm work is but a mere fraction of what it was! So, that is my perception. Theirs is another. Should ever the twain they meet, we could all be satisfied, I suppose.

The time has come for me to rest in order to be prepared for tomorrow.

Until then, good night.

Agnes.

Holy crow! A diary! Her diary! This was Agnes Walker's diary! This was amazing! Here it was! Her life, her family, her lineage – her entire story contained in the pages of this book. Corinne was beside herself with excitement. She had just struck gold!

Chapter Ten

Corinne stared down the piano.

It pathetically stared back.

She looked at the face of it. An instrument that was once solid, regal and beautiful was now merely a skeleton. She wasn't even sure where to go next. Perhaps the legs. They looked fairly sturdy and solid.

The case looked thin and weak. She wasn't sure if it would hold up or not.

Rather than risk it, Corinne planted herself on the cold, hard basement floor. She rolled the sandpaper around the leg and began pushing it up and down. Some of the paint was coming off, but it was difficult. Because of the intricate decorative design, the legs had thicker parts and thinner parts; some simpler areas, other more intricate areas. She figured for now that she should focus on the main bulk of it. Getting the majority of the paint off now would make her life easier when she was ready to tackle the more difficult areas.

As she continued to try to sand off as much of the drab, olive green paint as she could, she began regretting not buying the hand tool from the salesman that day that she bought the orbital sander from him. She may need to go back to the store now that she sees what she's truly up against.

Trying not to get overwhelmed or defeated, she sanded away for a couple of hours on those old piano legs. There was some improvement. It wasn't as much as she had hoped, but the wood was visible, and the progress made was clear and easy to see.

Dear Diary,

This morning, my beloved Chief was feeling quite frisky! Once he was let out of the stall he ran around the pasture and jumped and kicked wildly! He was feeling quite brisk and energetic. He made me laugh with his antics.

The students proved to be a bit challenging today. Perhaps because today was an unusually warm day both Chief and the children were zestful.

Most of the students settled down after a short while. Thomas was nearly impossible to keep quiet.

At one point, I decided to pull him aside. I reminded him of the importance of a good education. I spoke of the necessity of the information we are studying. I asked him what career he hoped to have as an adult. He said he hoped to write for a newspaper one day. I explained to him that the only way to achieve that goal would be to study well and for him to apply himself completely to his school work. Much to my delight, he returned to the classroom and continued as an ideal student for the remainder of the day.

I joined Margaret Begum for lunch. What a delightful lady she is! She is quite a happy soul. She is funny and jovial. I greatly enjoy her company. She is fast becoming my closest friend.

So all in all, it was a lovely day. It had some trying moments, but it ended beautifully. Now the time has come for me to rest in order to be prepared for whatever tomorrow may bring.

Until then, good night.

Agnes.

Corinne looked through old pictures of the house online. It was so interesting to see how it had changed over the years. Most of the photos were black and white, of course. She could only imagine what it really looked like back then.

She stopped suddenly. It was less than a skeleton in this picture. A few burnt posts and rafters remained. This was the damage done from that fire. When was that? 1864 or 1865, she thought. She could not believe the severity of it. A beautiful house was nothing but a pile of ashes. So much of the Walker legacy burned that day. It was sad. There were other pictures – images of the burned up crop fields and horse barns.

Wow. Just wow. This was unbelievable. It was tragic, really. She wondered if it hadn't burned down if things would have changed. If the family hadn't lost their palatial home, would things have been different? What would the house look like now? Would it still have hundreds and hundreds of acres? Would the town have had to sell it to that Mickerson guy because it was vacant for twenty years? What would have happened? What would have changed? Anything?

There was a slight chill to the crisp, early autumn air. The sun was shining brightly on the crimson colored leaves.

Margaret look up and all around as they entered the house. It was a farm house, but it was beautifully kept. It served as a nice home. "This is quite lovely," she said to Agnes.

"Thank you! It has become slightly more difficult to maintain since my parents have passed; I do the best that I can."

She admired the pristine woodwork and lightly colored walls. "Well I think it looks lovely. You have done a wonderful job."

Agnes smiled greatly. "Well thank you. I appreciate it, especially since it's coming from you. Thank you."

Margaret smiled back at her. "You are quite welcome."

Agnes felt awkward – almost uncomfortable. There was an air about Margaret that caused Agnes to feel nervous and excited. She shifted her weight and looked at the floor for a moment. She suddenly perked her head right back up. "Oh! There is one part you haven't seen yet! Would you like to meet the one man who has captured my heart? My dearest friend since childhood?"

Margaret was taken aback. "Most certainly," she said with trepidation in her voice.

"Come with me!" Agnes exclaimed. She grabbed Margaret's hand and ran with her out of the house and down towards a barn that was a short distance from the back of the house.

"You have a man living in your barn?" Margaret asked in between her deep breaths as she ran.

Agnes laughed heartily.

After a short jaunt, they reached the barn doors. With great enthusiasm, Agnes opened the doors.

Margaret stood at the door way.

"Go on!" Agnes encouraged her.

Margaret took one cautious step in. "Hello?" She called. Her voice slightly echoed through the barn.

She shrieked when a large chestnut horse head appeared out of one the stalls.

Agnes walked in laughing. "Margaret, this is Chief."

Margaret was still breathing heavily from her shock.

Smiling, Agnes grabbed her hand and walked her over to the majestic animal.

"Chief, this is Margaret."

As if he understood, he softly nuzzled Margaret's elbow with his nose.

Margaret studied him, taking in the sight of what very well could have been the most beautiful horse she had ever seen.

He was a rich chestnut color, with vibrant white patches. His mane was black, except for one patch of cream colored hair that rested above one small white spot on his neck. His eyes were big, deep, gentle brown eyes. He was tall and regal, just like Agnes. He had long white "stockings" on all four of his legs. His tail was also a mixture of black and cream hair.

"He's...gorgeous!" Margaret said softly.

"I'm glad you like him."

Again, Chief lightly nudged Margaret's arm.

"And he clearly likes you!" Agnes chuckled.

Margaret began to gently pet his face and nose. "What a remarkable creature!"

Agnes beamed. "Thank you."

The women were quiet as Margaret continued to pet and admire Chief.

Margaret turned her head slightly to look at Agnes. "Thank you for introducing me." She said softly.

"It was my pleasure." Agnes' face radiated with gladness and joy as she watched her new best friend with her childhood best friend connect.

Agnes Walker, Louisville. Corinne typed into the search bar. The same scant links appeared. What would happen if she clicked on images?

There were a few. Not many, but some. They didn't look like the pictures she had. Well, she hadn't seen anything like these yet.

There was a picture of the teachers at the primary school. Agnes stood taller than everyone else. Her dark hair was pulled back and up. Her eyes looked really light. Corinne wondered what color they were. How great would it be to see her in color?!

Her clothes looked dark and heavy. Again, it was hard to tell for certain.

She had high cheeks bones. Her features were strong, striking, and yet also elegant and feminine.

Next to her stood Margaret Begum. She was shorter than Agnes. She, too, had dark hair that was pulled into a bun. Her eyes were darker than Agnes', but they were gentle and not very dark. She had a round face, and very young features. She was a pretty and almost adorable lady. Her dress was long and dark.

Hattie McGowan was next. She stood slightly taller than Margaret. She donned the same hair as the rest, but she wore a large hat. Her dress was light in color. Both her hair and her eyes were light as well. She was rather plain, her features were sharp and harsh, and she looked very rigid.

Eleanor Smith was the last in like. She was the second tallest of the group. Her hair and eyes were also dark. Her features were very soft and feminine. Her dress looked black. She was tall and curvaceous. She was an attractive woman.

Staff and Faculty of the Louisville Primary School 1907 school year.

This was fantastic! She could put faces to the names she's read about in Agnes' diary. Corinne smiled. All of this was so fascinating and so...cool! She loved it.

There was a knock at the front door. Agnes glided over and opened it. Margaret stood on the other side.

"Hello! Welcome! Do come in," Agnes greeted her.

"Thank you," Margaret said as she came in.

"You're just in time! It's time to feed the birds."

"Birds?"

"Yes!" Agnes said gleefully. She skipped over to a small room. She stepped back and showed off four little bird cages. "These are my patients."

"Your what?" Margaret asked with a smile and a chuckle.

"My patients. Should any baby birds fall from their nests, or any little critters like rabbits or chipmunks become injured, I take them in. They each have their own little homes and I feed them and care for them until they are ready to return outside."

Agnes stood tall before the bird cages. She carefully placed seeds and water into each one, bending down to look at and speak to the little residents inside. A sparrow, a wren, and two finches each occupied their own little homes. Each one was clearly loved by her. She spoke gently and kindly to the tiny creatures. They chirped happily as they received their food and water from Agnes.

"My, you are magnificent!" Margaret whispered to herself.

Chapter Eleven

Corinne pulled a newspaper clipping out of the box.

Clarence Harrison Named Superintendent of all Louisville School District Schools.

August 23, 1908 – The Louisville School District has hired Clarence Harrison as the new superintendent of all schools within the Louisville School District.

Mister Harrison and his wife, Charlotte, came to Louisville from Elizabethtown.

He has extensive training and knowledge of education; he served as the principal for the Elizabethtown High School for the last seven years.

Mister Harrison's name may sound familiar as he is the grandson of Obediah Harrison, a well-known, wealthy land baron who owned most of Elizabethtown.

The Louisville School District is very pleased and excited to welcome Mister Harrison and add his knowledge and experience to our schools.

There was a weak knock at the door. That was peculiar. Agnes was not expecting any company.

She carefully opened the door.

She was pleasantly surprised to see Margaret standing on the other side.

"Margaret, my dear! Come in! It's a delight to see you again." Agnes smiled at her. "Can I get you anything to drink?"

"N-no." Margaret stuttered. She seemed nervous, anxious.

Agnes gently placed her hand on Margaret's arm. "Is everything alright?"

Margaret looked at the floor.

"Margaret?" Agnes softly asked. She looked down at Margaret and they both rose back up together.

"Agnes, there is something I need to tell you. I'm afraid, though. I fear the ramifications of my words. I fear how you may react."

"Margaret, I consider you a dear friend. I promise you this: you will not be judged for your words here."

"Dear, that makes you an angel. I am not sure whether it makes this any better or worse."

"Go on. Say it." Agnes placed her hand on Margaret's shoulder.

Margaret's dark green eyes grew softer and lighter. Her gaze held on Agnes for a few moments before she stepped away. She dared not look Agnes in the eye. Her sight fell upon the floor again. "Agnes." She took a deep breath. "I love you. I've loved you for a long while, unfortunately. I think about you incessantly. Your voice brings me much joy. The sight of you with your beloved Chief, or any of your small animal friends brings me peace. I treasure every moment we share. I have tried to dismiss it, disregard it, and ignore it. Alas, I cannot."

Margaret took another step backwards, getting further from Agnes. "So there you have it. My dark, dirty secret. I am madly in love with you, Agnes."

Agnes stood quietly for a few minutes. She stepped forward and placed her hand on Margaret's shoulder.

Margaret looked up at her and gazed into her crystal blue eyes.

"Margaret, I fear that I, too, have a confession to make." She paused for a while, breathing heavily all along. "I have often considered myself to be a solitary person. Having no siblings and losing my parents at a young age have caused me to become self-sufficient and independent. I had no one else to rely on other than myself. So I relied on no one. I took care of myself, and remained somewhat isolated."

Tears began to well up in Margaret's eyes.

"However, upon meeting you, I knew I had made a good friend." Her expression lightened. She turned to face Margaret completely. "As time has gone by, you have been proven to be more than that. Although I am very much a singular person, I find myself to be incredibly happy when you are present. Though I never expected to say this to anyone, I believe I am madly in love with you."

The tears rolled freely down Margaret's round face. "Really?"

Agnes smiled. "Indeed! I could not conceive of a life without you. You have found your way into my home and my heart. I look forward to seeing you at the school. I greatly enjoy your company when you visit. You always brighten my days and cheer up my spirit. The imagination of a life with you is sweet and magnificent."

"Oh Agnes! That is wonderful. Simply and perfectly wonderful!" Margaret grabbed and tightly held Agnes' hands. She paused, and her face dropped. "Though, what are we to do at the school? We could never let on..."

"And we shan't." Agnes reassured her. "There is no reason why we cannot carry on as we usually do. They already know us to be the best of friends. We need not act any differently, and they would never think anything has changed."

Margaret sighed a sigh of relief. After a few moments, though, her face again wrinkled into an expression of concern. "I do not know how to ask this. We are both ladies of good character. Neither of us has seen anyone previously, so I don't even know it all works. How are we to see each other, as other couples do?"

Agnes gently rubbed Margaret's hands that still rested in her own. "You are welcome here at any time, you know that. I also don't see why two ladies could not enjoy an evening out together. Friends join each other's company for coffee, or music, or what have you."

"I worry because I am living in my parent's home. I couldn't have you come around very often. Nor could I spend too much time away." Margaret lamented.

Agnes nodded her head. "Ah, I see.

"Well, I suppose we could see each other under the right circumstances. You may visit here as often as you like. Perhaps we could occasionally visit with your parents, though they will know us solely as friends. We may enjoy each other's company on a night out on the town from time to time. I don't imagine it will be as difficult as it sounds."

"What are we to do when..." Margaret could not bring herself to the say the words.

"This is my home. It has been in my family for generations. I have no reason to leave. My home has been and always will be open to you.

"When the timing is right, you could move here under the guise as a 'boarder.' This way no one would be surprised that you have come here since we have such a deep friendship, but we also are able give our relationship time to grow and blossom."

"Oh my sweet Agnes, you are so smart to think of such things."

"And you, dear Margaret, are such a joy." Agnes smiled. She gently lifted Margaret's hand and tenderly kissed it.

Dear Diary,

Today is the greatest day of my life.

Margaret came to visit today. She seemed scared, worried.

I asked her the matter, and with great hesitation she told me she loved me. I don't think the angels could sing sweeter than hearing those words from her.

For so long, I have pined for her, and kept my thoughts to myself. We have always thoroughly enjoyed our time together. We laugh like silly little school girls. We both enjoy the brightness of a sunny day, and the mystery of a starry night. As time has progressed, so have my feelings for her.

I thought I must have been mad, though. What woman falls in love with her dearest friend? I figured there was some kind of illness that was making me feel this way.

At first, I feared she was terminating our friendship. That would have easily killed me. Instead, she proclaimed her love for me!

Oh, it is so wonderful! I am happy and excited and exuberant. Words cannot describe my joy. Never in my life have I received such a wonderful gift as that of Margaret's love.

Oh joy! Sweet, wonderful joy. I feel liberated! I am not sick. There is nothing wrong with me for loving her. If it is an illness, then she has it as well! What a wonderful illness and I should pray that neither of us will ever be cured!

Look at me, rambling on and on like a fool. Perhaps I am one. A fool for Margaret. A fool for her love.

I cannot express enough just how happy and wonderful I feel at this very moment!

I should rest. I have to teach tomorrow. I fear that I am so joyful, I won't be able to sleep! Should that be the case, though, it would be the greatest case of insomnia that I could ever imagine. Either way, the sun shall rise and I will enjoy yet another day of loving sweet Margaret.

Until then, good night.

Agnes.

Chapter Twelve

Corinne looked at the piano as best she could. The dim light, and the shadows of the basement provided very little help as she looked at it.

"Hmmmm." She paced back and forth, staring at it incessantly. There were small, detailed areas that still clung to the nasty green paint.

Should she go back and get the Dremmel? It wasn't as if she was rolling in money that she could be spending it frivolously. She's already spent a good amount of money on it as it was.

It was so hard trying to do the intricate parts by hand, but right now, she really couldn't justify buying another tool.

She grunted in frustration.

With a sigh, she walked over to one of the difficult areas. She wrapped the corner of the sand paper over her index finger and began sliding it into the crevices. This was definitely not going to be perfect. Hopefully it would make enough of a difference that any green spots may not even be noticed.

She pushed with as much strength as she had to really dig in there and get that paint off. After a fair amount of time she pulled her hand back to see.

Not a great change. There was still plenty of green that was quite visible.

"Argh." She grumbled. This wasn't working. It was never going to work. Why did she even start on this stupid project anyway.

Corinne threw down the sand paper and stood up. She took two steps away from the wretched piano, and stopped.

There was something pulling her, trying to get her attention. Something about that stupid piano was calling to her.

She slowly turned around.

It was still a pathetic, dilapidated old piano. It retained very little of its original charm. And yet, she could see the beauty underneath the beast. She could tell this was her diamond in the rough. It was old, it was ugly, and it was hers. She was probably the only person in the world who could ever see it for the gem it really was. In some weird way, she had a connection to it. For whatever reason, she was brought to this piano, and it to her. She couldn't give up now.

"Fine!" She said begrudgingly to it.

Corinne walked back, picked up the sand paper, and started sanding the same little piece again.

Agnes knocked on the door. Her heart was pounding. She could hear footsteps running towards her.

Margaret opened the door with a grand smile. "Agnes!" She exclaimed. "Welcome!"

"Hello my dear." Agnes smiled back. She couldn't greet Margaret the way she wanted, but her eyes told Margaret exactly what she was thinking.

"Come in!"

Agnes walked through the door and was immediately greeted by Margaret's father. He extended his hand out to her.

"You must be Miss Walker."

"I am." With an equally strong grip, she shook his hand.

"Our daughter has spoken quite highly of you. It is a pleasure to finally meet you. I am Horace. My wife, Lenora, is inside."

"It is very nice to meet you, Mr. Begum. Your daughter is a wonderful educator. It has been quite pleasant to work with her."

"Come join us." He said guiding them both into the house. "I must say, I do pity you. With your parents gone and you needing to tend to a large house all alone. I would imagine it cannot be easy."

"I thank you for your sympathies, Mr. Begum. I suppose it's alright. I'm used to it, so it doesn't bother me much."

"That speaks highly of your character, Miss Walker. I admire you for your strength and courage as a woman."

"Thank you."

They walked into the parlor where Lenora lounged with a book. She stood up to greet them. "Hello. Are you Miss Walker?"

Agnes offered her hand. "I am. It's a pleasure to meet you, Mrs. Begum. Your daughter is a lovely woman."

"Oh thank you!" Lenora chuckled; she shook Agnes' hand. "Please join us."

They all sat around the room. Agnes sat across from Margaret. She loved being able to look directly at her, but it was so difficult to maintain this façade.

"Margaret, Darling, why don't you play for us?" Horace asked.

"Oh yes! Please do!" Lenora agreed.

"Play?" Agnes asked.

"Oh Margaret is a wonderful pianist. She is quite remarkable, I must say." Lenora answered.

"May I hear?" Agnes inquired.

Margaret smiled. "I'm a tad nervous having an audience, but I would hate to disappoint you." She smiled at Agnes. She slowly got up and walked to a piano on the other side of the room.

Margaret sat down, took a deep breath and began to play.

Beautiful music began to fill the room. Margaret closed her eyes and swayed with the music.

Agnes and Margaret's parents also got swept up in the beautiful melody. Each note was precise and perfect. Her music was gorgeous and warm and breath-taking. Her music was infallible.

Once it was over, everyone slowly opened their eyes.

Margaret's cheeks were flush with color. She smiled brightly at Agnes.

Agnes could not help but smile back. "That was beautiful. Thank you."

"You are more than welcome."

"That was quite lovely, as usual." Horace said. "Thank you, Margaret."

He stood up and turned his attention to Agnes. "Come now, would you care to join us for supper?"

"I would be honored. Thank you, sir."

He reached out to help her up. He then followed suit with Lenora.

Margaret walked up quickly to stand next to Agnes.

They both smiled at each other with big, bright, beautiful smiles.

"Come, then." Horace said. "Off to the dining room."

The quartet all walked out into the dining room.

Corinne reached deeply into the envelope. There was a small batch of notes all tied together with a string.

She was nervous, but also excited to see what they were.

Sitting on the floor, she spread them all around her like some little paper barricade.

She unfolded the first paper.

My Dearest Margaret,

I wonder if your eyes should ever fall upon this note. For you see, I have tremendous feelings and tremendous fear about what I am going to say here. If you should see it, I hope your eyes are open and full of joy. If not, I shall die a sad, lonely woman.

Margaret, I have come to fall in love with you. I dare not speak such words. Not even I can fully comprehend the severity of them. Not even you can fully comprehend the joy of them. You have been a dear and wonderful friend. You are a beautiful woman with a stunning soul. I am forever grateful for having not only encountered you, but to have this precious friendship we share.

I know how precious – and how fragile – this kinship is. I am struggling with preserving its fragility while being boldly and bluntly honest. How does anyone achieve such a balance?

Margaret, should you reciprocate, I would have a joy and a love that would supersede all words and all time. If you should not, I pray that you are not offended by these words and would simply leave me to live in solitude.

My inner most demons now have resided on this very piece of paper. Only time can decide whether or not your eyes should fall upon them.

I love you with all of my heart and soul,

Agnes.

How sweet! Agnes' first love letter to Margaret. She wrote it before Margaret ever came out to her! They were destined to be together. Corinne couldn't stop smiling.

On to the next letter.

Oh sweet Margaret! How you have made me the happiest woman today.

Never would I have imagined that a woman like you could ever fancy an old hag such as myself. But you have! You told me so yourself. Hearing those words escape your lips was akin to hearing the angels in Heaven sing. What a beautiful and wonderful moment. One I shan't forget; one for which I am ever eternally grateful.

Dear sweet, wonderful woman. I cannot promise you a life of ease, but I can promise you a life of love, comfort and solidarity. My heart, my soul and my life are yours now and always.

I love you with all of my heart and soul,

Agnes.

Corinne could not fight the giant smile that crossed her face. These letters were so sweet and sincere. These were absolutely wonderful!

Corinne grabbed another note randomly.

My Dearest Margaret,

89

Pianissimo

Happy Valentine's Day! You are the greatest valentine I could ever wish and hope for.

You bring me such joy. You are a gift to everyone who knows you. I am so incredibly fortunate to have you by my side. This life we share far surpasses my greatest dreams. Thank you.

I will love you until the end of time, I swear it!

I love you with all of my heart and soul,

Agnes.

Corinne clutched the letter to her chest. These were priceless! She absolutely adored them! She had to read another one!

My beloved Margaret,

So many years have passed, and yet you remain the most beautiful woman to walk the Earth.

You never cease to amaze me; I fall increasingly in love with you each and every day. I trust you with my life. I can say anything and still be safe. You share my joys and pains, my triumphs and my frustrations. You keep me safe and warm every night.

I do so wish we could have the same freedom as others. Sadly, we must keep ourselves private. But know this: though I can't always show it, you were, are and forever will be the love of my life.

Happy anniversary to my "Darb Dame!"

I love you with all of my heart and soul,

Agnes.

Oh! Corinne could not get enough of these! They were simply wonderful! She gathered them all back up and tied the string around them again. She picked herself up off the floor and ran upstairs with the batch in hand. She was going to have some great reading tonight!

The door was open, but Agnes was nowhere to be found inside. Margaret began to look around the outside of the house. "Agnes?" She called out.

After a few moments, Agnes came up from the back field. "Margaret! It's so wonderful that you're here! I didn't expect you would visit."

Margaret planted her feet solidly on the ground, hoping it would make her feel more brave. "I have come to visit with a purpose."

"What might that purpose be?"

She leaned in towards Agnes and murmured. "I would prefer it if we were to go into the privacy of your home."

"But of course!" Agnes ran to the door and kept it open for her.

"Thank you," she whispered as she walked in.

Agnes closed the door. "What troubles you?"

"I have no troubles, I have a request."

"Oh? What might that be?"

"Agnes," she sighed. "I would very much like to...be your..." She hesitated. She took in a deep breath and spat out the word, "boarder."

Margaret clasped her hands together. "I love my parents very much, but I also love you. As any young woman, I am in need of some privacy and freedom." She reached over and grabbed Agnes' hands. "Moreover, I want to be with you. The more time I spend with you, the more time I crave. I cannot live like this any longer. I love you, and I need you, Agnes. Please let me live with you. Please. It would make me the happiest woman alive. Please take me on. Please let me be...your wife."

Agnes took a wider stance. "Are you sure this is the decision you want to make? You do understand the potential consequences of this."

"Yes. I am willing to risk that for a lifetime of happiness with you."

"You realize this has the potential to jeopardize your career, you relationships with friends, family, and the townsfolk. Do you understand there will be rumors and talk of us? Are you willing to risk your reputation with the town? Are you sure you are willing to give all of that up and risk all of those awful things just for me?"

Margaret's face lit up. "Yes! A million times yes. I would do anything and everything to be with you. I would rather be hated for sharing my love and my life with you than to be accepted into social circles." Her eyes pleaded with Agnes.

"Do your parents know of your wishes?" Agnes firmly asked.

"I told them that I thought I'd best be on my way to independence. I said that since I had no suitors, it would be a safe and practical decision to live as a boarder with you until my circumstances otherwise change."

Agnes nodded her head. "What was their reaction?"

"They thought it was a splendid idea."

"They did?"

Margaret smiled. "Yes."

Agnes turned with her back to Margaret. "Well then I think there's really nothing to discuss." She turned back around. "You shall move in here and we will live happily ever after." Agnes smiled and winked.

"Oh Agnes! You certainly know how to make a woman happy!" Margaret embraced her.

"My dear, sweet, Margaret. It is you that makes me incredibly happy."

They held onto each other tightly, soaking up this exquisite, perfect, moment.

Chapter Thirteen

Corinne grabbed a bunch of photos and several papers out from one of the envelopes in the box. She sat on the floor and spread them all around herself.

She grabbed a newspaper clipping first and looked at it. She couldn't help but laugh.

Mrs. Elizabeth England's rose bush has totaled one hundred buds this year. She is offering some of the buds and flowers for sale at five cents per piece, Mrs. England may be visited at 100 Nightingale Lane.

What a great little article in the newspaper. It was so quaint. She wished modern day news read like that.

She turned the paper over to see what was on the other side.

Miss Agnes Walker has taken in Miss Margaret Begum as a boarder in her home at 38 Locust St. Both ladies are educators at the primary school.

So this was how they were able to live together. Margaret was a "boarder." And the town would believe that they were simply two lonely spinsters living and working together. Surely people would find that to be acceptable. Granted, it was odd for women not to marry in those days, but it couldn't have been too bad. Would anyone really judge them for being old maids? Why would they? Corinne wondered. It couldn't have been too awful. As long as they were able to keep their lives private, there was no reason for anyone to bother them.

She had to stop herself for a moment. She was becoming so engrossed in their lives. She was so curious about them. She had a connection to these women. She shared their house, their piano, and now the photographs and memories of their lives. She wondered about how the townspeople viewed them as two old maids living together. Every little bit encouraged more curiosity. She couldn't get enough of these girls.

The girls. The new girls in her life. Like she called Millie and Mollie the girls, but they were people. Deceased people, but still people.

Yeah, she thought to herself. Another pair, another set. Millie and Mollie were the girls, and Agnes and Margaret were also the girls.

Margaret came into the house. Things had been moved. The house was in a minor state of disarray.

"Agnes?" She called out. She moved very reluctantly. She was afraid Agnes had been hurt...or worse. "Agnes?" She called out again.

"Oh Margaret! I wasn't expecting you quite so early!" She rushed into the kitchen and corralled Margaret away from the door that led into the living room.

"Agnes, what on earth is going on? Are you alright?"

Agnes smiled. "I'm fine, dear. Couldn't be better."

"So what's all this commotion about?"

"Well, my love. You see the yuletide season is upon us."

"Yes it is."

Agnes wrapped her arm around her. "Since it is our first holiday together, I wanted to be sure you received a present far better than you could ever imagine."

Margaret's face expressed confusion, fear and excitement. "And what might that be?"

"Come with me. Close your eyes."

Margaret hesitated before finally closing her eyes.

Agnes led her by the hand into the living room.

After several painfully long moments, Agnes quietly spoke. "Here."

Margaret opened her eyes.

A gorgeous mahogany wood upright piano sat before her. It was brand new and perfectly pristine. It was immaculate and impeccable. Margaret's breath was taken away. "I..." she stuttered. Her eyes welled up with tears. "I cannot thank you enough."

Agnes smiled warmly. "It is my pleasure, Margaret. You are a wonderful pianist, and I wanted you to have an instrument that was worthy of your talent."

Margaret stood dumbstruck.

"I hope you like it."

"Oh Agnes! I love it! I am beside myself with joy!"

"That makes me happy." Agnes replied. "Merry Christmas."

Margaret turned to her. Tears still streamed down her face from her green eyes. "Thank you!"

Agnes opened the door. "Welcome to my humble home, Mister and Missus Begum!" "Merry Christmas!"

"Merry Christmas, indeed!" Mister Begum replied as they entered the house.

"This is quite a lovely house." Missus Begum said. "You really maintain all of this by yourself?"

"I do," Agnes said as she escorted them into the dining room. "Not by choice, mind you. This is my lot in life, though; I do my best to accept and maintain the responsibilities."

"For you to take care of this entire home and Margaret as well, I feel guilty. It is we who should be hosting you for Christmas dinner." Lenora Begum replied.

"Oh no! Margaret is a delight to have here; it is really our pleasure to have you here as our guests." Agnes smiled.

Margaret lightly skittered into the room and hugged her mother. "Oh! Mother, there is another reason as well. You absolutely must see the divine gift Agnes gave me for the holiday!"

Lenora grabbed her hands in excitement. "Oh? Do tell!"

"Actually," Agnes interrupted them. "My thought was that perhaps after dinner we could...use the gift and sing carols."

"Oh that is a splendid idea!" Margaret said.

"Please, everyone sit. I shall return with our dinner in just a moment." Agnes walked into the kitchen.

They all sat around the table. Dishes of corn, potatoes, biscuits, yams, asparagus, and stuffing were already placed on the table.

"My dear, it seems you have a wonderful friend in her." Mister Begum said.

"Oh I do! She is just splendid. She is a good soul. She has taken such good care of me. It's wonderful to board with such a dear friend. We enjoy each other's company: we play games or knit together. It is simply lovely."

"Nor do you need to worry about men. Not all men, just men of poor character." Horace added.

"Indeed! Yes, I certainly do feel safe." Margaret paused. "I'm sure that if a gentleman was to call upon either of us, the other would respect their privacy. We can also ensure that the other isn't being duped by an unsavory man."

"Hearing all of that makes me feel much more comfortable with this situation." Lenora Begum said.

Agnes entered the room with a large turkey.

"Ah! That looks wonderful!" Horace exclaimed.

"Thank you." Agnes placed the turkey in the middle of the table. She came around and took her seat.

"Let us pray," Horace said.

They all joined hands, closed their eyes, and lowered their heads.

"Come! This is what I wanted to show you!" Margaret grabbed her mother's hand and led her into the living room.

Lenora Begum gasped. "Is this...?"

"Yes!" Margaret squealed with excitement.

"Oh my! That is a wonderful gift. How awfully kind of her!"

"Oh I know, Mother! I play it and we'll sing together. It has been absolutely wonderful!"

Missus Begum walked around the instrument. "It's an R. S. Howard! That is quite impressive."

"Oh! It is just a wonderful instrument, Mother. I love it!"

Her mother smiled. "I'm sure you do."

Mister Begum entered the room, followed by Agnes.

"Is this what all the fuss is about?" He asked.

Agnes smiled and slowly nodded her head. "Indeed."

"That is quite the hefty gift, Miss Walker."

"It is, but it is well worth it. A house is not home without a piano." Agnes smiled.

"Agreed!" Missus Begum said.

"It was my pleasure, really." Agnes turned to Horace. "I have no family, no siblings. It is therefore rather easy for me to spoil your daughter as such."

Mister Begum smiled. "Don't do that too often." He chuckled.

"Oh I shan't." Agnes smiled back. "Come now, shall we sing carols?"

"Indeed!" Missus Begum said. "What shall we start with?"

"Silent Night?" Margaret asked.

"That is perfect!" Missus Begum agreed.

"Wait, though!" Margaret pleaded.

"What's wrong?" Mister Begum asked.

"Father, could you possibly take a photograph of us with the piano? I would love to cherish this moment forever."

"I would love to, but we don't have photographic camera!"

"I do," Agnes said gently. "If you wouldn't mind helping me to move it, Mister Begum."

"Not at all."

They left; Margaret looked at her mother.

"Isn't it just wonderful?"

"It is," she said quietly. "Miss Walker seems to have some money. She also seems to spend it frivolously."

"Oh no! Not at all, Mother. The camera has been in the family for a while. Yes, she bought the piano, but that is the first luxurious item I have ever seen her purchase. Her family was certainly well to do. It is nice being able to enjoy that."

"Not too much, now." Her mother said. "I'm not quite sure I like the sound of that, either."

"It's really not as it seems. Yes, I enjoy the fact that she was able to purchase the piano and give it to me as a Christmas present. In no way do I take her or her money for granted, I promise you that."

Agnes and Mister Begum came back in carrying the camera, the plate, and a large stand.

Carefully, they put it all together and set the plate in the camera.

Margaret sat down and looked up at Agnes. Agnes stood beside the instrument and smiled down at Margaret.

After several long moments, the bright light went off, creating a blinding white flash.

Horace then carefully placed the camera with the plate in it off to the side.

"Oh thank you, Father!" Margaret said.

He walked over to rejoin the group. "Anything for my little girl," he smiled.

"Now, let's start caroling!" Agnes said.

Margaret turned and faced the piano. Her fingers danced and skipped over the keys with light perfection.

Corinne walked down the wide aisle looking all the way up. The amount of wood and lumber in here was insane. The ceiling was easily over twenty feet high. And lumber was stacked from floor to ceiling. How on earth was she ever going to find what she needed – and then get it down?

She just happened to glance at a guy as he walked past her.

"Excuse me!" She called out.

He stopped, turned around and looked at her. "Can I help you, miss?" He said in a derogatory way.

"Yes, I'm looking for some mahogany wood."

"You want mahogany? What do you need mahogany wood for?"

"A piano," she said hesitantly.

His brow furrowed. "A piano?"

"Yes. I am restoring a piano. It's missing some pieces, and it was originally made out of mahogany."

He continued to have a cynical look on his face. "Seriously?"

Corinne walked closer to him. She dropped her arms, cocked her head and narrowed her eyes. "Seriously," she said sternly.

"Alright." He rolled his eyes. "Come with me."

He led her to where the mahogany wood was stacked. The only thing that could be heard were their footsteps echoing down the aisle.

"Here ya go," he said with apathy. "How much do you need?"

Oh crap! She hadn't thought of that. She hadn't measured out the piano yet. She figured she'd do that once she got home. She tried to quickly and nonchalantly look at the stickers with the different measurements.

"Well..." She tried to stall him. "I know it needs to be 5/8ths thick." Thank goodness she had remembered that from something she had just read on the internet. "And..." She looked at the labels desperately. "Forty eight inches in length by forty eight inches wide."

He stared at her.

She looked again and pointed at the label again. Then she pointed to the large piece of lumber. "This right here."

"Okay. You want one."

"I'll need two," Corinne said, hoping she was saving herself from having to come back here again.

He glared at her one last time. "I'll get these and meet you at the check-out line." He grumbled.

"Okay. Thank you." Corinne whipped around and gladly walked away from him.

"What was I thinking?" Corinne grunted as she tried to pry the giant sheets of lumber out of her car.

"Do you need some help, miss?"

Corinne turned around.

A man, probably in his mid to late sixties jaunted across the street towards her. He had thick curly brown and grey hair. Black wire-framed glasses rested highly on his long, strong nose. His light blue eyes sparkled.

"Hi! I'm Rich. Rich Adams." He extended his arm.

Corinne shook his hand.

"My wife Susie and I live across the street there. I've seen you when you moved in. Looks like you don't go out too much. I wanted to say hi, but you seem like a private person, so I didn't want to bother you."

"Oh," Corinne lightly chuckled. "It's okay. I'm Corinne."

"So what are you doing with all of this lumber?" He asked as he heaved the giant sheets of wood out of the hatch back.

"Oh!" She hesitated. Everyone has treated her like she was crazy. Would he, too? She decided to give it a shot. "Fixing a piano."

"A piano? Is there still an old piano inside?" He asked with tremendous curiosity.

"Yeah," she felt her face wrinkle into an expression of confusion with a bit of skepticism. "Why? How do you know about it?"

"I grew up here – in my house across the street. I remember Miss Margaret playing the piano. She gave me lessons for a short while."

"She did? You knew Margaret and Agnes?" Corinne was becoming giddy with excitement.

"Yeah. They were both very nice. They were quiet ladies, kept to themselves. Just like you. My mother wasn't too fond of them. She thought it was odd that they were two spinsters living together, staying away from most people. But my father and I always thought they were nice."

Corinne was in shock. This was amazing! "Wow! So, can you tell me more?" Then she realized he was still standing there, holding the two big sheets of lumber. "Oh geez! I'm sorry. Come on right down with me."

She guided him down to the basement through the old outside entrance. She quickly grabbed the string and pulled. The light cast a yellow haze over the room. As best it could, the piano lit up.

"Oh wow!" He whispered. He placed the planks right next to it. He knelt down and began examining it. "I can't believe it's still here. It looks so sad. What is this?" He leaned in closer, adjusted his glasses and began examining the areas that weren't completely sanded yet.

Corinne came over and knelt down beside him. "It was painted green. Like drab, olive-army green. Who did that or why, I will never understand."

"Yeah, no kidding." He looked at her with great confusion. "Oh wait a minute. You know what? I bet that was from some stupid college kids. When Mickerson bought the place, he rented it out to college kids. I wouldn't be surprised if they did that."

"Oh, maybe." She softly relied, suddenly putting the pieces together. "I've been trying to sand it and clean it up. I still have a little ways to go yet."

"It's not bad, though." Rich said. "You've done a great job so far. Do you need tools? I've got plenty."

"I bought a sander."

"That's good. What about all of this detail work?"

"I was going to go back and get a hand tool – like a Dremmel, the guy said."

"Don't waste your money. I've got one. You can come by and borrow it any time. I have saws too, for when you need to cut these. I'd be more than happy to help, if you want."

"Thank you! I appreciate that. Since you knew them, and know how to do this, I might just take you up on that."

"Please do!" He said emphatically. "It would be my pleasure. Plus, Susie makes some of the best homemade chocolate chip cookies you'll ever have!" He smiled at her.

"That's really nice. Thank you again."

"No problem. Talk to you soon."

Rich walked away, and Corinne stayed in the basement for a few minutes longer, smiling. She had made not just a friend, but someone who knew the girls as well. This piano project had unexpectedly taken on an entirely new meaning.

Corinne handed Rich another photo. "Look at this one."

"Wow," he chuckled. "It's so funny seeing them like this." He waited for a moment. "How did you get all this?"

"It was down here, in a box by the piano."

"Really? They just left it here?"

"It seems that way. I can only assume Dick Mickerson just put it all together and left it down here."

Rich shook his head. "I don't know about that. He was never one to really...preserve anything. Know what I mean?"

"So who would have done that?"

"I don't know." He replied. "Someone cared at some point over the years."

Corinne just looked at him. Slowly, her eyes fell back down on the photographs. There was one. Both women were dressed to the nines, and the piano could be seen in the background. "Wow," she whispered.

Rich turned his attention to the photograph in her hand. "Boy, they were both beautiful ladies."

Corinne looked up. "Yeah they were! Do you remember them looking like that?"

"No. I was just a young boy. I didn't look at them that way. To me, they were just two little old ladies. Now being the age that I am, I know they were anything but old!" He chuckled.

"What were they like?"

"They were nice enough. Like I said, they kept to themselves. They died when I was eight, so I don't really remember much."

"But they left some kind of an impression on you."

"They did. I think now more so just because of their age and their introverted-ness. I would love to have known the women behind the myths and rumors."

"Myths and rumors?" Corinne asked.

"Yeah. There has always been some local folklore about them. Some people thought they were witches or were involved in something strange like that."

"Really?"

"Well sure. They were teachers, so they were certainly involved in the community. But they weren't a huge presence per se. They kept to themselves, and mostly stayed in the house. They rarely went out, and you almost never saw them really socialize. So people would gossip.

Rich chuckled for a moment. "Even my own mother. She really didn't like them. My father didn't mind. It was actually quite a point of contention between them. I remember them arguing when they started talking about having my sister and I take lessons. Mom wanted us to learn how to play, but definitely not from them.

I'm not quite sure how my father won that one, but we got our lessons from Miss Margaret.

Mom was so mad! She wanted nothing to do with them. She was as much a part of the rumor mill as everyone else."

"Really? Wow! What was it like at home when you took lessons and your mom didn't like them? What did she say? What else did everyone else in town say?"

"Like I said, for my family, it was a point of contention between my folks. My mother was pretty much mute about it when we go to our lessons and what not. She wouldn't ask us about them, and we were not supposed to talk to her about them. That was her best way of dealing.

"As far as the general rumors around town, Miss Agnes always took in little critters like birds and chipmunks and took care of them. The people who didn't really like her would say that she would sacrifice the animals or that she was just plain crazy. She was also the last in the lineage of a famous and wealthy family. So people wondered what she did with the money, or how weird she was coming from a prominent family and not acting like it at all.

"Miss Margaret was a little more liked. Miss Agnes could be blunt, cold and even authoritative. Miss Margaret was much warmer and kinder. I think people pitied her more than they did Agnes. Don't get me wrong, they were both social outcasts, no questions asked. They were outsiders; I think they actually liked it that way! Overall, I think Agnes was a little more coarse and would rub people the wrong way. Margaret was just seen as weird, not mean."

"Did any people like them? Were the missed when they died?"

"Honestly," Rich started. "Not really. Margaret's family was there for her funeral, and it seemed it was more out of obligation than anything. A few people from the school showed up, but my parents told me that no one really came to their funerals. It was like the town didn't care about them."

"Wow!" Corinne could not even begin to fathom something like that. "That's so sad!"

"It is. It's a shame. I think they were really nice and just misunderstood."

Corinne sighed a sad sigh. That was a really sad story. She was starting to like the girls. They seemed nice so far. Why did people look down on them? Why wouldn't anyone come to their funerals? "That's just awful."

"I know." Rich shrugged his shoulders. "So you can see, it really makes you think and wonder about who these women really were."

"You're not kidding! As I go through more stuff, I will let you know."

"That would be really nice, Corinne. I really appreciate that. Thanks!"

She smiled at him.

"Well, I'd best get going for now. But we'll talk again soon."

"Yes!" Corinne replied emphatically.

"See you later." He smiled, slowly stood up and left.

Corinne loved having someone to share all of this with. Rich was a great guy and he was becoming a good friend.

Sunbeams weaved through the leaves of the trees as the sun began to greet the world. Margaret's hands danced lightly over the keys of the piano. This was her morning meditation. Never was she at peace the same way as when she made music. She and the piano had an understanding of each other: something that no one else could comprehend, but everyone could appreciate.

Agnes came down the stairs with a smile on her face. She stood silently in the doorway, quietly absorbing the sight and sound of her beloved.

This was their morning ritual. Margaret played and Agnes quietly admired. It was a peaceful, soulful way to start every day.

"Miss Walker?" The tiny voice of David Butler just barely caught Agnes' attention.

"Yes, David?" She turned around.

"Would you...?" He stuttered. "Could you...?"

Agnes leaned in towards him. "Do you need help, David?"

His little brown eyes dropped to the floor. "Yes, ma'am."

"That's alright. There's nothing to be ashamed of. Every person needs help from time to time. No one person knows everything, David. So we can all learn from each other."

His eyes looked at hers with a soft, genuine look that only a child could have. "Really? Is that true?"

Agnes smiled. "It is indeed! Now, what can I help you with?"

"It's the literature." He stumbled on his own words.

"Are you having a difficult time reading it?"

"Yes, ma'am. It's rather difficult to read and some of the words don't make sense."

"Alright, then." Agnes started. "Can your father help you at home?"

David's eyes fell to the floor again. "My daddy died."

"Oh, I'm sorry to hear that." She paused. "And your mother?"

"Mama can't read."

"Oh, I see." Agnes said gently. "Is it just the two of you?"

"We live with my uncle Billy now. But he doesn't like children."

Agnes paused, trying to think of a resolution. "Well, I think I have the perfect solution for you."

"You do?" His little face lit up.

"I do. You will need to ask your mother first to see if she will approve of this. I say you and I stay after class for a little while every day, and we go through the book together."

"You would do that for me?"

"Of course, David! You're a good boy, and you have a lot of potential. You could be anything you want."

"Really?"

"But of course! You can succeed at anything you do. I would like to help you succeed. So we will read together and I will be happy to answer your questions." She paused. "Please be sure to ask your mother and make sure she doesn't mind if we do this for a while, alright?"

"Yes! Thank you so much, Miss Walker!"

"You're welcome, David. I'll see you tomorrow."

"See you tomorrow!" He ran out of the room as quickly as his little legs would let him.

Margaret came walking in. "He's quite the little sprinter, isn't he?"

Agnes chuckled. "Indeed. He's a good child, though."

"Who is that?"

"David. David Butler."

"Oh!" Margaret replied.

"You know him?"

"I know of him. His father died working on the railroad a few years back."

Agnes thought for a moment. "Oh! Now that you say that, it does come to mind."

"Yes. Poor boy. His mother was forced to move in with her brother who is nothing but a drunkard."

"How are they able to maintain the home?"

"Lord only knows, Agnes. I pity them, though. I really do."

"That is quite tragic."

Margaret nodded. "It is."

There was a short, sad, slightly awkward silence for a few moments.

Margaret looked out the window. "Now, shall we get back home before it gets dark?"

Agnes smiled and stood up. "I suppose we should."

They walked out of the schoolhouse together.

Chapter Fourteen

"We would like two tickets for Gone With the Wind, please." Agnes said.

"Here you are, ladies." The young gentleman handed them each a ticket.

They both thanked him before going into the movie theatre.

"I am so excited!" Margaret exclaimed. "The word is this is a wonderful picture."

Agnes smiled at her. "I'm sure it is."

Everyone turned around and glared at them when they walked into the theatre. They both smiled weakly. They found two isolated seats towards the back.

It wasn't until they were completely settled in their seats did the other audience members pry their gaze off of them.

They could hear them all mumbling and whispering to each other.

Agnes looked sadly at Margaret. Here they were simply trying to enjoy a nice evening out, and they drew attention to themselves. Not by doing anything, simply by being themselves. Didn't friends go to moving pictures together? Why were they seen as such an oddity? Agnes quietly sighed.

Margaret took Agnes' hand and placed it in her own. She smiled at her.

Agnes' face reflected an expression of love, and also of fear.

"It's alright." Margaret whispered.

Just as she sat back in her seat, the movie began to play.

Throughout the epic film, they both caught people staring at them; they sometimes heard people talking about them. Were they that much of a sideshow that they drew their attention away from a moving picture? This was insanity! They were there for the same reason as everyone else: to simply enjoy the picture. They led such a quiet, private life. And yet here they were stealing the spotlight from this amazing film. Agnes shuttered a number of times due to the glares that were directed her way.

Once the movie was over, Agnes and Margaret scurried out of the theatre as quickly as they could. Even as they briskly walked, they could still hear people talking about them.

"What the hell is wrong with you? Why are you so afraid? Is it because you know you're odd? You know that you're not normal?" A man shouted at them.

Their pace quickened.

They could hear his steps. They were loud and strong. It sounded as if he was getting to them very quickly.

They walked even more quickly.

His footsteps sounded as though he was right behind them.

Agnes stopped. Still holding Margaret's hand, she turned around.

She was right. A very tall man stood there.

"Sir, I wish to know the nature of your complaint with us. What have we done to possibly offend you?"

"Look at you! Two spinsters living alone together. You work together. You are always seen together, and yet you are rarely out of your house."

"And there is a problem with that?"

"Well it certainly seems odd. Why would two adult women walk into a moving picture together holding hands?"

"Dear sir, perhaps it is in your best interest to find out all of the information before making any assumptions. My eyesight is poor. Especially at night. So yes, my dear friend, with whom I work, is here holding my hand. She is guiding me back to my house. Now if you will excuse us, we would like to walk the remainder of the trip alone." She paused for a second simply to breathe. "Good evening."

She turned around and they quickly resumed their quick pace back to the house.

Corinne lay in bed. Ugh. She couldn't sleep. It was too hot. She couldn't get comfortable. The television was too distracting. Her mind was racing. It was just past two in the morning. Why even bother at this point. Sleep was not coming her way.

So, what should she do to keep herself occupied? She was not going to work on the piano. It was too dark down there, and she really had no desire to work on it anyway.

She could go downstairs and get a drink. Maybe she'd do that. But then what?

The love letters! This was the perfect opportunity to read more of those. She climbed out of bed and raced down the stairs.

She poured herself a large glass of milk and situated herself on the couch. She pulled them out and untied the string. She grabbed her first letter.

Dear Margaret,

I must confess that I am afraid at times.

We are so often viewed as strange and peculiar. Is there something wrong with us? Are we truly that bizarre? Is our relationship not natural, as so many would have us believe?

I am quite torn, to be perfectly honest. I adore you with every fiber of my being. I cannot – and will not – deny that. I have always loved you, and I shall love you long past the end of time.

It's our abnormality that confuses me. Are we the only people in the world who live and love as we do? That couldn't be possible, could it?

I worry because of how misunderstood we are. I worry because of how hated we are by Clarence Harrison. I worry about our safety and well-being.

Please, don't misunderstand me. I love you and would never leave you or the life we have together. Not even for a "safer" façade of marrying some man. No. I would much prefer to be hated with you than to not face the stares, glares, rumors, or gossip.

I just hope and pray that we are safe and that we will be welcomed into Heaven as all of our friends and family.

Know that your safety and well-being are of my utmost concern. I shall never allow anyone to harm you in anyway. You are my wife, my treasure. For as long as you'll have me, I will remain by your side through life.

You are my light, my love, and my world. I will love you infinitely.

I love you with all of my heart and soul,

Agnes.

Corinne stopped and thought about that for a moment. These women lived in fear. They were nearly exiled from their neighbors and community. They were deemed as odd and unnatural. They may not have publicly slapped the homosexual label on them, but everyone knew. Corinne always thought their gay life was kind of weird, but they weren't bad people. They were teachers like many women. It wasn't as if they abused their students or tortured their neighbors, or anything. There was no reason for them to be tormented like that.

"That's just plain stupid," she said to herself. Let them be weird. She didn't necessarily agree with being gay, but she wouldn't bother anyone who was. "Whatever, I guess." She mumbled. With a sigh, Corinne opened the next letter.

My Dearest Margaret,

I cannot believe how quickly the years have passed. I feel as though we have just met, and yet here we are ten years later!

These have been the greatest ten years. I could never imagine a life without you. You are the sunshine on my darkest days. You are my joy. The happiness you bring me is insurmountable. I could not survive even one day without you here.

I know that I can be difficult, and I so greatly appreciate your patience, kindness and love for me since I truly do not deserve it.

Thank you for being the most wonderful person in my life. Words will never describe the depth of my emotions. Time will never end the duration of my love.

I love you with all of my heart and soul,

112

Agnes

Awe! That was sweet! Corinne smiled. She liked that. She pulled yet another letter out from the pile.

My Dear, Sweet Margaret,

Life is not always as pleasant as we would like it to be. We lose friends and family members. We feel pain and sadness. We feel hurt and disappointment. For as much good in the world as there is, there is an equal amount of badness.

I understand your pain in losing your mother. I will never forget the day I lost my parents. I realize that these words probably seem hollow to you right now. That is only to be expected. I encourage you to hold onto this note. Read it and read it again. Read it, read it, and read it until it resonates and restores your soul.

This is a dark, sad, tragic time for you and your family. You have all of my love, support, and sympathy. Whatever you want or need is yours. Simply say the word.

You will get past all of this one day. You may never fully be the same person you were before her passing. I have never been the same since my parents died. That is alright. No one expects you to be the same. No one expects you to act as if nothing happened. Life will continue on. It always does. However, it is a different life now. Sadly, it will always be different. Years from now, tears will still find their way into your eyes. That is alright, too.

Your mother was a wonderful woman. In the few times I have been in her presence, I have admired her and greatly enjoyed her company. Her beautiful, wonderful daughter is a perfect mirror of her, and will carry on the family legacy beautifully.

I love you, Margaret. I always will. When it seems that all hope is lost and that life no longer has meaning, do your best to hold onto my love. It is always there. It will never change or end. My love and I are with you for eternity.

I wish I could remove your pain. That would be such a wonderful thing. Unfortunately, I cannot. I can do my best to do and be everything that you need now and always.

Pianissimo

You have all of my love and sympathy.

I love you with all of my heart and soul,

Agnes.

Corinne wiped away a tear. She placed the letters on the coffee table. She needed a break for a little while.

"Must we really go?" Margaret asked as she placed Agnes' over coat on her.

"It's a not simply a function for the school, it is the holiday party."

Margaret made her way around Agnes and pulled the coat so it rested flawlessly on her shoulders.

"We need to make an appearance." Agnes continued. "We can certainly keep it brief, though." She smiled down at Margaret.

"Good, because I have no desire to spend time with the likes of Clarence Harrison!"

Agnes chuckled as she placed Margaret's coat on her. "I don't blame you one bit, my love."

Agnes now stood before Margaret; she pulled and fixed the collar until it was perfect.

"My friend," Margaret winked as she corrected Agnes.

"My friend like no other!" Agnes smiled a devilish smile. She suddenly pecked Margaret on the cheek.

Margaret squealed.

They laughed and fell onto each other.

"See? We are having a wonderful time here. There's no need to leave." Margaret said in between chuckles.

Agnes fought to catch her breath. "I know. As I said, it shall be a brief appearance. And then we can resume our horse play."

Margaret stood up. "You're no fun."

Agnes straightened her coat and dress. "I know." She huffed. "Let's come along now. The sooner we do this, the sooner we can come back home."

They walked briskly up the street; thankfully the function was only a half a block away.

Margaret stared up at the sky. "It is a lovely evening." Her voice was quiet and breathy.

"That it is!"

"All the more reason to not lose time being with the likes of those people."

Agnes laughed heartily.

The walk was a quick but pleasant one. When they entered the doorway, they were bombarded with the stench of alcohol, many faces, and very loud conversation. Clearly, the booze had been greatly enjoyed by most everyone there.

"Oh dear." Margaret whispered to Agnes.

"This shall be an incredibly brief visit." Agnes whispered back.

"Agnes! Margaret! So nice of you ladies to come join us!" Raymond Wilson said.

"Thank you, Raymond." Agnes replied. "I see it is quite festive here."

"Too much for my taste. People will do as they see fit. It certainly won't be my problem come tomorrow morning."

"Nor ours!" Margaret concurred.

"Smart girls." Raymond flashed them a quick but bright smile. "That is why you are the best two instructors on staff!"

"Oh Raymond, you flatter us." Agnes replied.

"Only enough so that I can't get in to trouble." He joked.

The trio laughed.

"Well, it is good to see you ladies here. I doubt any of us will be here for too much longer. Enjoy your evening!"

"You as well, Raymond." Agnes said.

"Shall we leave, then?" Margaret asked with great excitement in her eyes.

"Soon." Agnes whispered.

"Whom else is here that we need to impress?"

"I just want to be sure we are noticed. I would fear the possible gossip that could arise should they think the two introverted teachers refused to come to a function for the school which employs us."

Margaret looked at her.

"You know they say enough as it were. A few members of the administration have their eyes on us. We mustn't give them reason to dispose of us."

"And how do you know of this?"

"Raymond. Thankfully, he is able to see past the rumors and to appreciate us for our work."

"Is it really that serious?"

"He says that it very well could be – that there is definite potential for that to occur."

"Oh my word!"

"Indeed, Margaret. Though I would rather not spend the time here, we cannot afford for anything to happen."

"Understood." Margaret replied.

"Margaret!" Clarence Harrison shouted from across the room. He was quite inebriated. He staggered and stumbled his way over to them.

"Hello, Mister Harrison." Margaret said quietly.

"Hello." Agnes said.

"Good to see you here. And please, call me Clarence."

"Alright, Clarence." Agnes said.

Without paying any attention to Agnes, he wedged his way in between them. His back was towards Agnes.

"You know, Margaret, you really are quite a darb dame. I must say it surprises me that you haven't married yet. A man would be a fool to pass up an opportunity with you!"

"Oh, well, thank you." Margaret feigned sincerity as best she could.

"Well I mean it!" He poked her in the arm as he spoke. "You are quite a darb dame. Why, I regret marrying my wife! She isn't nearly the darb dame that you are!"

Margaret took a step backwards. "I am sure she is very darb, as you say. I don't think she would be very pleased to hear you speak like that."

He leaned forward. "That will be our little secret, eh? What she doesn't know won't hurt her." He nearly fell on her.

She pushed him so he stood upright again. "Are you sure?" Margaret asked, hoping that she might be able to reason with a drunken man.

"As certain as I am that you are a darb dame!" He smiled a weak, drunk smile.

"I see. Well, I thank you kindly. You have a wonderful evening, Clarence."

"It would certainly be better if I was to go home with you." He began to try to put his arm around her.

Margaret quickly grabbed his hand and shook it. She fought desperately to fake a smile. She inhaled deeply. "Again, I thank you. It's late, I'd be best be home now. Good bye."

From behind Clarence, Margaret grabbed Agnes's hand and led her right out of the building.

"Dear God! Can you believe that man?" Margaret asked in disgust.

"I'm not quite sure what was worse: his drunkenness or his limited vocabulary. I don't think I have ever heard the term 'darb dame' as much in my entire life as I did this evening." Agnes chuckled.

"His poor wife."

"Indeed! She has married quite a filthy hog, hasn't she?"

"First off, I could not even imagine being married to him even in the most basic of senses. Add to that his tom cat behavior, and my heart goes out to her." Margaret said sympathetically.

"I suppose. She married him for some reason, though." Agnes quietly argued.

Margaret was silent as she thought for a few moments. "My guess would be for his family's fortune."

Agnes nodded her head. "Agreed. So I suppose it can't be all that terrible. Theirs isn't a marriage based on love. It is based on what is most important to them: themselves."

"That is a pathetic existence, if I may be so bold."

"I agree it is, Margaret."

Margaret leaned over and spoke softly. "For as much as we need to be careful, I greatly enjoy the life we have together. I could never imagine being with someone for whom you have no respect. I'd rather live a quiet life happily next to you than to ever marry someone for any sort of convenience."

They stood outside the front door to the house.

"That, my dear," Agnes said quietly. "Is the exact reason for which I love you. You are a good, honest, sincere person. Someone who is true to themselves and the people around them. And," Agnes paused. "You are a darb dame!" She laughed as she ran into the house.

What a young, beautiful, regal girl she had been. Even at a young age, she had such distinctive features. Strong, but feminine. She was tall and lean. Her dress enveloped her narrow shoulders and caused her lanky body to disappear underneath it. Though not smiling, there was a look in her light eyes. A look of pride; a look that reflected her soul.

Next to her stood a most handsome horse. His long lean neck reached up to the sky. He held his head proudly. His dark mane rested beautifully on one side. He wore his large dark and light spots as if each one was a masterpiece: a true work of art. Though the picture was only black and white, Corinne could imagine his amazing colors leaking through the picture.

Agnes and her beloved horse, Chief, 1899 the back of the photo read. What an amazing image. What an amazing moment. Someone's companion, most treasured friend – her soul mate and her soul captured together in one split second on film.

Corinne smiled a small smile in thinking of how happy Agnes must have been with her beautiful horse, and to have this impeccable moment captured permanently in time.

She gently placed the picture off to the side.

My Dearest Margaret,

Today is a new and beautiful day. That is reason enough for me to write this letter and to tell you how deeply I love you.

You are the most amazing person I have ever known. You are smart, witty, and absolutely beautiful.

Thank you for giving me the great blessing of sharing a life and love with you. It means more than words could ever describe. Please know that there isn't one moment of my life that goes by where I am not thinking of you.

You are my light and my love. I shall love you past the end of time.

I love you with all of my heart and soul,

Agnes.

"Margaret!" Clarence Harrison shouted down the hall.

She looked up. She had been gathering her belongings. Now she clutched them tightly as he approached her.

"Hello, Clarence." She weakly greeted him. Her heart began to pound in her chest.

He came closer and closer.

She stepped back a couple of times until she was stuck in the corner of the room.

"I'm glad I was able to speak to you before you left."

"Yes. What is it? What can I do for you?"

"I think you and I should conference. Sometime soon. I think it would be best if it was simply between us both. I don't want other staff members to feel...slighted by what I would like to tell you."

"Slighted? How so?"

"I wouldn't want things to be seen as favoritism. You are clearly good at educating, and I want to be sure that is recognized, but without any complications from anyone else."

"I'm not quite sure I follow."

"Well," he leaned in closer. "I have a proposition for you that would benefit us both." He rubbed her cheek with his short, fat finger.

"And I have a proposition for you." Agnes' strong voice came from the doorway.

Clarence stood up and spun around. "Hello, Miss Walker. I do believe that none of this affects you in any manner."

Agnes walked in towards him. "I beg to differ, dear sir. Whatever affects my co-worker, my boarder and my friend absolutely affects me." She stepped forward. "Now do tell us. What exactly is this proposition?"

"As I said, Miss Walker, I don't believe this should be any concern of yours."

Agnes glared at him. "I shan't leave until you have explained yourself to us both."

"Miss Walker!" He growled.

She stood firmly in her place, staring him down.

The three stood in an awkward, tense silence.

After several uncomfortable minutes, Clarence's posture changed.

"So be it. You should be fully aware that your behavior here will be addressed."

Agnes sneered. "I fear nothing, little man. You'd best be on your way."

Clarence pushed his way past Agnes and quickly left the room.

Margaret caught her breath. "Thank you." She whispered.

"I don't like that man." Agnes turned and looked out into the hall. "I certainly do not like how he has treated you. Something must be done."

"What, though? It is not as though we can express to him – or anyone else – the true nature..."

"Regardless of that, you should feel safe and protected in your place of work. That behavior is unacceptable."

"He said the same of us." Margaret replied.

"Should he ever consider to threaten us with the loss of our jobs, his actions will brought to light."

"Agnes, I cannot thank you enough for your courage. I must admit, however, that he is in a position of power. He could have us..."

"Fear not, Margaret. We have done nothing wrong. Besides, we have Raymond on our side. He knows what rubbish Clarence is."

"Are you sure? People speak behind our backs. You know that we are looked on as social outcasts for being who are. I don't think our presence here would be missed."

"My dear." Agnes said as she wrapped her arm around Margaret. "You are an amazing educator. They would be foolhardy to lose someone like you."

Margaret smiled. "Well, I think you're a tad biased!"

Agnes laughed heartily. "Perhaps. There is no need to worry about that, though." She winked at Margaret. "Let me walk you home."

The women left the school house arm in arm.

Dear Diary,

My dislike for Clarence Harrison only continues to grow. He has harassed Margaret incessantly. He searches her out like a bloodhound. He refuses to leave her be. He started from one or two small incidents per week to daily to now haranguing her multiple times per day. It's disgusting. He has no respect for her at all. He does not understand the concept of boundaries. He certainly knows no rules of being a gentleman.

He's been watching us as we leave, as well. Initially, we could see him watching from his office. Then he would follow us to the door. Today, however, he walked behind us all the way to the house. We tried to act normally. He could be seen from the corner of our eyes. He kept some distance, but not nearly enough. He has me quite frightened. He knows where we live now. He continues to push and pursue Margaret. What is to stop him at this point? At any point?

121

Pianissimo

Margaret has told me that he has also become more threatening as well. He has threatened her job, and her public image. He has told her that it is not normal for two women to live together. He said it goes against God and nature for us to not marry or bear children. He says the nature of our relationship is not right and that he will expose us for the heathens that we are.

Neither of us can afford to lose our jobs, moreover though, I am concerned about our welfare. I don't even worry about his threats to "expose" us publically for not living "in a normal and natural manner." It's our safety, and hers more so, that worries me. She does not deserve to be harmed in any way. She has done nothing wrong. She is a kind, sweet, good woman.

Ever since that holiday party, he has grown into a monster. It's deplorable.

I do not understand why this must happen. Neither she nor I have caused harm to anyone. We have not lied or stolen nor hurt any one person. Not in the least. We simply want to live a quiet life together. The details of our relationship are the business of no one else but ourselves. We do not exhibit our affections publically. We make certain to keep our private lives private, and to focus solely on education when we are working. Why is it that we are seen as bad or ungodly or as some kind of a threat to Clarence Harris?

I long for a utopia where all people are free to live simply as themselves with no threat, anger or issue from anyone else.

As another night closes, all I can do is pray for our safety and well-being. Perhaps one day, someone will understand our plight. Perhaps one day, all people will live in happiness and safety.

Until then, good night.

Agnes.

Chapter Fifteen

"Do you still play?" Corinne took a sip of water.

"No, not really. I have a piano at home, we really only use it at Christmas." Rich replied. "How about you?"

"No," Corinne replied with disappointment in her voice. "I wish had kept it up. But I was offered a college scholarship for soccer, so I gave up music to play soccer. Wouldn't you know it, in the beginning of the season I hurt myself. It had rained right before the game, so the grass was really wet. I slipped. When I did, I tore my ACL. And as I was falling, another girl came behind me and she fell. When she fell, her one leg slipped out from underneath her and kicked the back of my knee tearing my meniscus as well."

"Ouch!"

"Yeah," Corinne lamented. "So here I am years later with a messed up knee and no athletic career."

"Hey," Rich interrupted her thoughts. "If you keep going with this thing, though, you could start playing again."

"Yeah. I'd like to. I think it would be fun to play again." She paused for a moment. "You know, one of the things I love about the piano is that it can angry and percussive, or it can be gentle and melodious."

"Very true!" He agreed. "It is certainly a multi-faceted instrument. It's so classic. I love that it's still used today. It has really stood the test of time."

"Yeah! I'm really sorry I gave up on it."

"Well you didn't give up on it completely. Look at you now! Not only are you interested in taking it up again, you're bringing one back to life!"

Corinne thought for a few moments. She had never really considered that before. Yeah, she did want to revisit her musical past and try playing again. And she really was bringing this one back to life. It was old, decrepit, disheveled, dismantled – it was essentially dead. Her intention wasn't necessarily to bring it back to be useable again. She just wanted to honor Agnes and Margaret. She just felt that it shouldn't continue to sit and rot in a basement. It had once been a beautiful, majestic gift. She couldn't let it remain like that in such a poor state. She was really just bored and this had given her something to do. She never realized how much more this was – how much deeper this whole project really went.

"Yeah," she whispered. "I guess you're right."

Raymond walked into the room. "Agnes, may I have a word with you?"

"But of course! Please do come in."

He came into the room cautiously.

"Agnes, we must talk." His voice was deep and quiet.

"Your tone concerns me." She replied.

He took a deep breath. "There have been some rumors and talk that are disturbing at best."

Agnes walked over to him. "Is Clarence Harrison involved?"

Raymond lightly nodded.

"Sir, I can assure you that any words that have come from that man's mouth are false."

"I'm sure of it." Raymond agreed. He leaned in towards her and spoke softly. "I worry, though. You and Margaret are sometimes seen as..."

"Odd? Bizarre? Queer? Peculiar? Abnormal?" Agnes rattled off the adjectives quickly.

He sighed. "I'm concerned that they might find cause or reason to release one or both of you."

Agnes looked him right in the eye. "Clarence Harrison cornered Margaret and proceeded to harass and proposition her. He threatened us both when I came in and stopped him."

"He propositioned her?"

"Indeed. He used his physical presence to threaten her as well as his words, telling us that we had just jeopardized our positions here by refusing to cave into his demands. Clarence Harrison is not a safe man, Raymond. Nor is he professional, courteous, respectful..."

"I understand." Raymond cut her off; he straightened his posture. "Say no more, Miss Walker. I shall tend to the issue." He placed his hand on her shoulder. "You shouldn't fear anything. I will put this all to a rest."

He began to walk out the door.

"Thank you!" Agnes called out.

He turned and looked at her. His deep brown eyes were light with warmth and understanding. He smiled and nodded his head before leaving.

Dear Diary,

Poor David Butler. He is a good little boy, but he struggles greatly. I have been reading with him and working with him diligently for a while now. The boy is not stupid, not by any means. When read to and spoken to, he is able to grasp the concepts of literature. My concern is that as he ages, he will not always have people who can give him the time and patience he requires.

He is such a good little soul, and I worry about his future. Should he continue to struggle in his education, I fear he may not be able to make a decent wage. Unfortunately, he may be forced to work some form of manual labor and potentially come upon the same fate as his father. I pray that isn't so. I will do all that is within my power to help the poor boy. I shall keep him in my prayers for years to come.

As for more pressing matters, I do feel something is amiss at the school. It seems as though there is much gossip stirring around. I'm sure Clarence Harrison has some role in all this. I don't mind the stares and glares. We've dealt with that long enough that we are immune to it. I don't suppose I'm really all that bothered by the rumors, either. My concern is Clarence Harrison and his capacity to hurt or ruin Margaret in any way. I don't wish ill upon him, but I would be delighted for him to simply disappear.

That probably makes me a terrible person for saying that. I don't wish to be awful, I just worry about Margaret. I will do everything within my power to protect her.

As you can tell, it has been a very long, strenuous day. Thankfully, this day has come to a close. Time to rest up and see what adventures tomorrow has to offer.

Until then, good night.

Agnes.

My Dearly Beloved Margaret,

Times are trying right now. There is much tension in the air at the school. We are both watched as if we were criminals of some sort.

Clarence Harrison's behavior has been increasingly horrific. His actions towards you frighten me greatly. I worry about your safety, and I fear for our positions with the school.

Though things seem to be dark right now, I want you to know how deeply I continue to love you. Clarence can try with all of his might, but there is nothing short of the hand of God that could ever change my love and devotion to you.

In the darkest, most frightening moments, please carry this with you. I love you, and I always will.

We are unable to see the future. We do not yet know the outcome of this horrendous situation. I have faith, however. I have faith in God, and faith in us. No one can ever truly tear us down or apart. We are both strong, resilient women. Women who know how to live and love. Women who are quite capable at their jobs. Women who live a good, honest, quiet, devoted life. I truly believe we shall overcome this trial.

We may not fully be able to see the light at the end of this darkness, but it is there. Take my hand. Walk with me, and together we will enter the light.

I love you more than mere words could ever say. You are God's greatest gift to me, and I shall treasure you always.

I love you with all of my heart and soul,

Agnes.

Joshua Flynn was a young, intelligent, articulate man. He had rich, dark brown hair. He was a handsome man with strikingly bright green eyes. He started the hearing. "There have been some questions regarding the behavior of Miss Begum and Miss Walker. We are here to address any questions, concerns, rumors, lies, or otherwise." He paused momentarily. "I would like to hear first from Mr. Harrison."

Clarence Harrison stood up. "I must be blunt. I apologize if my language offends anyone.

"The truth of the matter is, I am concerned about the behavior and lifestyle of these two women. They are quite inseparable. Neither is married. I question the nature and manner of their relationship. I understand that women have need to be around other women; that they spend time together sharing recipes and exchanging house-hold information. This is far greater than that, though. They live together, dine together, work with each other and walk with each other day in and day out. Tell me: is it normal for women of their age to be unmarried and childless? It is not as if one or both is a widow, or even a divorcee, God forbid. No, neither has wed. Ever. Their lives are deeply interwoven. The type of relationship these women share is concerning, suspicious and ungodly. I shudder at the thought of the witchcraft and other deviant behaviors in which these women engage behind closed doors."

Joshua stood up. "Mister Harrison, though we understand the nature of your concerns, I fear that you might be directing this into a topic or issue which we cannot address. Would you be able to discuss other situations or concerns at the school?" He asked.

"They both take concern in the other's business." Clarence continued. "I was having a private conversation with Miss Begum recently when Miss Walker loudly interrupted us and refused to leave. This was not a matter affecting her at all, but our conversation was forced to an end due to her lack of respect for me.

"Both women have been rather coarse in their interactions with me. They are not pleasant people, by any means. I really have to question whether or not two rude, introverted spinsters can be good educators."

Margaret and Agnes looked at each other.

127

"Is there anyone else who would like to express similar or other concerns?"

Their neighbor, Lacy Adams, rose to her feet. "I would. I am a neighbor of these ladies, and I share the same concerns as Mister Harrison."

Joshua stood to address her. "Your name, miss?"

"Lacy Adams." She turned toward the board members. "They keep to themselves. Miss Walker can often be found wandering outside talking. I don't know whether she is talking to herself or to some little animals or something. Either way, she certainly appears mad.

"They socialize very rarely. I find that to be quite peculiar. Have they no friends? If so, why is that? Is it by choice that they are reclusive? Or is it because they are not normal and regular folk simply cannot maintain any kind of friendship with women who are so unusual?

"They are an odd pair, and are rarely seen without the other. Neither has ever been seen in the company of a man. I, too, wonder about what goes on in that house behind closed doors."

She straightened up. "My greater concern, though, is for the children. What kind of a message are we sending to our children by allowing recluses like this teach them? Please tell me: how does it benefit the students to be learning from people who simply are not normal? My children are growing quickly and are bound to have one or both of them as a teacher at some point. Then what? They learn that it is acceptable to differ from social standards which we all know to be best for everyone? I do not want my children to learn from them. Their lifestyle disturbs me; I can find no benefit to the students by keeping them on as teachers."

She quietly sat back down.

"Anyone else?" Joshua asked.

Raymond jumped up. "I, for one, would like to stand up for these pillars of our community."

The group of people in the room all gasped, groaned, and expressed their discontent.

"Indeed, they are quiet, introverted ladies. I, too, find it peculiar that neither has started a family as of yet. That being said, however, there is something to say for the depth of their friendship."

He angled himself towards them. "They have the greatest kinship I have ever seen. They genuinely care about one another. They don't have husbands to care for them, but they both care for each other. Their friendship is solid, genuine. Theirs is a relationship that we should all try to emulate. They may be single women, but they have a tremendous sense of love, compassion, consideration, and even family for each other. You certainly cannot disregard that."

"If they are capable of such love, devotion and dedication, they most certainly are not bad role models for our children."

He turned back to the board members. "I can tell you this, as well. We need not worry about them wandering about and performing unbecoming acts. These women are upstanding. You won't find them doing anything that is unladylike. They abstain from alcohol and they keep away from sinister characters."

He leaned forward heavily on his arms which grasped the empty chair in front of him. "No, we have not seen them in the presence of men. As odd as that might be, it does also prove that neither is a hussy or a floozy. They are women of dignity. Both come from wonderful families, and they continue to uphold their families' reputations."

He straightened his back. "Personally, I would rather my child learn from someone who leads a quiet but pure life than someone who does the opposite. I hear you asking what kind of role models might they be. A nun is a woman that has never married; nuns are treated with tremendous respect and consideration. Now, Miss Walker and Miss Begum may not have become nuns, but with their behavior being akin to that of nuns, I feel that they are excellent role models. Theirs is a message of a good, clean, quiet life. There is nothing shameful there. I would be honored if my children were to learn from either of these wonderful women." He sat back down and smiled at them.

The room had taken on an entirely new emotion. It was disturbingly quiet. They eyes that had once chided them now exuded a more gentle expression.

"Ladies, would you like to say anything?"

Margaret and Agnes looked at each other for a moment. Margaret slightly nodded her head.

Agnes stood up. "I would, if I may.

"I can understand people's concerns since we are not married. I realize that we simply do not follow the normal social standards. I can appreciate a parent's concern for the image and impact that may have on their child. I can promise you that we both do our best to ensure that our pupils are not solely receiving a good academic education, but that they are also being taught social graces, proper behavior, and the like."

Agnes angled herself towards Raymond. "Mister Wilson is an intelligent man, and also a man with very high standards. I can assure you that if there was any question of our character or our abilities to teach, he would have disposed of us immediately."

She turned to face the board members again. "As he said, we do live quiet, private lives. We do not partake in excessive alcoholic drinking – actually, we do not drink at all. We do not fling ourselves at any man who happens to cross our path. Rather, we maintain our femininity and our dignity. We would rather be old maids than to dishonor ourselves by simply settling for just any man.

"Now, getting to the topic at hand. Mister Harrison is absolutely correct regarding that one incident where I interrupted his conversation with Miss Begum. I will not, however, go into detail about the nature of that conversation. Mister Harrison is a married man and is in an important position. I dare not sully his reputation nor jeopardize his marriage. I will tell you that if any of you were to fall upon a conversation such as that, you would have acted similarly as I. It was a situation that was best ended at that very moment. So I did."

She paused when she saw the board members writing down notes of what she had just said. She regained her focus, and then continued. "I can assure you, I have nothing but respect for every person in this room. I have equal concern for all of you. I would not want anything to befall any of you. It was for that same reason that I interrupted their conversation that day. The topic of that discussion was one that had potentially serious and harmful ramifications for both Miss Begum and Mister Harris."

She took a deep breath. "Say what you will, but I chose to act out of concern and respect. Again, out of respect, I shan't go into detail. My intention was out of concern and consideration that day, as it is today at this very moment. I am sure you are all able to understand that." Agnes looked around the room, and then at Joshua. "I believe that should suffice. Thank you."

She carefully lowered herself back into her seat.

"Thank you, Miss Walker." Joshua said. "Is there anyone else?"

The room sat silently.

"These are all things we shall take into consideration." He continued. "Obviously, these are matters that cannot be taken lightly. We shall consider all of the viewpoints expressed here this evening before making any final decisions.

"I would like to thank you all for your time and participation in this matter. A final decision will be made shortly; when that time comes, you will all be made aware of that decision."

After lengthy consideration and debate, the Louisville School District has decided to maintain the positions for Miss Agnes Walker and Miss Margaret Begum.

Their character had been in question, as well as some alleged disrespectful and unprofessional behaviors.

Opinions from both sides of the matter had been heard and taken into consideration during this deliberation.

Though both women are quiet and somewhat reclusive, no criminal or inappropriate behaviors or actions could be found for either of them. Their positions with the school district are being upheld.

This matter shall not be brought up again as per Chairman of the Board, Joshua Flynn.

Chapter Sixteen

Clarence Harrison walked into Agnes' classroom and slammed the door shut. She whipped around in fear.

There was anger in his eyes. He stomped over to her and pressed her right into the corner.

"Listen here," he grunted. "I don't know who you think you are, but this nonsense is over."

She tilted her head away from his hot, odiferous breath. She closed her eyes.

"I don't know what you're up to, but I won't have any more of it." He said through clenched teeth.

"I am a woman simply living my life and doing my job." She replied coldly.

He slammed the wall next to her with great force. "You're a liar!" He shouted. "What kind of demonic deviant are you? Do you think we don't know? Do you think we don't see? How stupid do you take us all to be? It's as clear as day! You're an evil person, and everyone around here knows it."

She looked him right in the eye. "Tell me, what constitutes evil? Is it the fact that I was orphaned and forced to be a self-sufficient woman? Is it the fact that being the sole survivor of my family, I needed to manage a farm house by myself? Is it the fact that I am a good teacher? That I spend time with my students and help them to succeed? Is it that fact that I am a well-educated woman? That I am eloquent, articulate and well-versed? Is it the fact that I am equal to you in height? Or is it the fact that I am simply more well-liked than you?"

He sneered. "So help me God, woman! I don't know what you're up to, but I will put a stop to this!"

She swallowed hard, but maintained her composure. "I would be very cautious of what I say and do, if I were you."

She held her head up, just slightly over his. "The ultimate reason for your loathing of me is my relationship with Miss Begum. You see me as being in the way – an obstacle blocking you from your prize."

She lowered her head and stared him right in the eye. "There are some problems to that, though. First and foremost, you are a married man. For whatever reason, some poor soul has committed herself to you." She paused, and lifted her head again. "Perhaps your vows are not as important to you as they are to others, I don't know. What I do know is that I am certain that your wife does. I am also certain that Miss Begum respects and understands the importance of such vows and would never put herself in a position where anyone's marriage could be torn apart."

Agnes lowered just her eyes, and she glared at him. "Secondly, Miss Begum has absolutely no interest in you. Were I not alive and you unmarried, you would still be unable to get to her. There is no interest on her part at all. So really, this is all simply a moot point."

She stood up straight, and stepped forward, forcing him to take a step backwards. "Let me say this as well: you are very fortunate that I bit my tongue as much I did at the hearing. I could have easily dragged your name and reputation through the mud. I did not. Being a better person, I only intimated at it."

She scowled down at him. "There very well may come a point, though, when I do open up and the world sees you for who and what you really are. You are on very thin ice, sir." She paused to take a deep breath. "Should you want to jeopardize your marriage, your career, and your reputation, then by all means, please proceed with this behavior." Her eyes narrowed. "Otherwise, watch every word that escapes your mouth. Watch every step and ensure that you are not walking into a dangerous situation.

"Do not forget that the board will not revisit your complaint. This issue is over as far as everyone else is concerned."

She stood up straight. "I know you would love to believe I am a witch of some sort, or that I am simply evil in nature. I hate to disappoint you, but I am neither. What I am is a strong, intelligent woman who refuses to be silenced by a small, ignorant man."

He squinted his eyes and leaned forward. "You are the one who needs to watch their every move. As God is my witness, I will have you removed from this school district!

"You are a witch! Everything about you in unnatural and ungodly. I hope you burn in hell."

The door to her classroom suddenly opened. Both Clarence and Agnes turned around.

Raymond stood in the doorway, and Margaret was behind him.

"Mister Harrison, is there a problem? Might I be able to help you with something?" Raymond asked.

He waited for a moment. Then Clarence slinked over to Raymond. "There is, actually, Mister Wilson." He paused. "I came here to greet Miss Walker since I had not seen her all day. I certainly did not want to appear rude. So I came here, and Miss Walker began to say some very inappropriate words. She also acted in ways that are unbecoming to a lady. I felt trapped as she attempted to seduce me: a married man!"

Raymond began to walk around the room.

Margaret scurried over to Agnes; she stood with her shoulders rolled in and her head hung low. She grabbed Agnes' hand, and held it tightly.

"I have worked in education for many years. My mother was a teacher, and I was raised in a family that strongly encouraged education." Raymond started. "Over the years, I have met many people. All personalities; children and adults. Scores of people and scores of characters.

"I do have to say, though, that working here in the Louisville school district has challenged me in ways I never could have imagined."

He paused as he continued to walk around the room with no specific path. He cleared his throat. "Never have I encountered such questionable and shady characters. I am appalled at the dishonesty, manipulation and unethical behavior I have seen."

Clarence smirked.

"Mister Harrison," Raymond continued as he still wandered about; he wasn't even looking at Clarence. "You have brought shame and embarrassment to this school with your complaints and actions. As if conducting yourself unprofessionally isn't bad enough, you have humiliated us in front of the entire city with that hearing! Do you understand the gravity of such dishonor? Can you even fathom the severity of the consequences from your behavior?

"I have watched you become severely inebriated at many, many functions. I have watched you act inappropriately towards both Miss Begum and Miss Walker. I..." He paused. "I need to be perfectly frank. I am disgusted by your words and actions. I am disappointed in the quality of your character – or lack thereof, I should say. You have been the source of tremendous stress and strain, not solely for me, but for many of us.

"I do not understand the origin or cause of your hatred for these two ladies."

He stopped right in front of Clarence. "Mister Harrison, I think it best that you find employment elsewhere. We shall no longer tolerate or ignore your unprofessional, inconsiderate and unbecoming behavior. I am asking you to leave the premises immediately."

Clarence's face dropped and turned a sick, pale color. "I...I..." He stuttered.

"There really isn't anything left for you to say, Mister Harrison. Please leave now." Raymond said with a stronger, deeper, more authoritative tone.

Defeated, Clarence Harrison slowly shuffled out of the room.

There was a heavy, uncomfortable silence. Raymond, Agnes, and Margaret did not breathe until after Clarence left the room.

"I..." Margaret started.

Raymond looked at them with sympathy in his eyes. "I am terribly sorry, ladies. I do hope this remedies the situation for you.

"I would love to speak with you further on this matter, but I must get home to my wife and family. I will see you both tomorrow."

Agnes nodded her head.

"Thank you," Margaret squeaked.

Raymond walked out of the room.

Agnes looked down at Margaret. She could no longer fight the emotion. Tears began to stream down her face.

"Oh Agnes!" Margaret said softly. "I am so..."

"You need not say anything, my dear. I would like to simply go home. I want to be safe in the quiet and security of our own house."

"Indeed, then. Let me take you home."

Dear Diary,

I continue to revisit the events of today. My mind simply cannot stop running through the scenario time and again.

I'm not even sure what to really make of it. Clarence is such a peculiar fellow. He was always a bit of an obnoxious fool, but he seemed harmless.

At that Christmas function, he was quite inebriated. I am actually surprised he remembered any part of it. He was rude and forward with Margaret to say the least. Again, we – or at least I – attributed it to the alcohol.

That was the night everything changed, though. After that, he became increasingly dangerous. His assertiveness, his harassment of poor Margaret, his behavior, his demeanor: everything changed, and for the worst. For over a year now, he has continued to grow in his belligerence, anger, and hateful behavior. It simply grew and grew.

I thought the hearing was everything coming to a head. Lord knows it was difficult enough. It was such an ordeal. I also expected everything to be finished once the board made their decision.

I suppose since he didn't fancy their decision, he was going to press further. And that he did.

I don't understand how a man of such little character – I am going to stop myself there for a moment. That is exactly the problem. He is a man of little character. He has no dignity, no refinement, no professionalism, and certainly no courtesy! Such insanity this was. I am still shaking my head over the matter. Truth be told, I wonder if I shall ever be truly able to wrap my head around this.

It brings me pause to think. I've always feared for us: for our safety, our normalcy and the like. Is such treatment justifiable? Are we really such horrible monsters? Do we really deserve such hatred and resentment? Is what we are such a terrible, atrocity of an existence that this was necessary? Is Margaret such a despicable soul that it was necessary for him to be so imperative to her and harangue her in this manner?

We mean to cause harm to none. Our intent was never to bother, disturb or upset anyone. We simply wanted to live a life that was suitable for us. Are we wrong for loving each other?

I pray we are not. She is such a wonderful human being. I am so blessed to share my life with her. I could not imagine living any other way. It would be a façade for either of us to marry a man simply because that is what society tells us to do. Would it be better to be liars than lovers?

I suppose I shall never know the answers to these questions. All we can do is carry on with life as usual.

With that, I bid this day a wonderful adieu. I am happy to be rid of it. Tomorrow promises to bring sunshine and blessings.

Until then, good night.

Agnes.

Corinne stared at Agnes' perfect penmanship. It was sad that these were her deepest thoughts. She was so concerned that there was something wrong with them. That she thought this idiot Clarence had every right to treat them as such.

"No," she whispered. "You didn't deserve this." No one should have ever been as tormented as they were by him. That's not right.

So what if they were gay?

Corinne stopped herself. So what if they were gay? She had never really thought of that before. She didn't really know any gay people. She always thought it was kind of weird. Not necessarily bad, but definitely weird.

Yet, here she was reading the diary of a lesbian who lived a century ago. And she doesn't seem weird. She's not some angry, man-hating lesbian. She just loved her Margaret. She loved Margaret for who she was, not what gender she was.

Is that what this has been about all this time? Like interracial marriages: it's about who the person is, not what they look like.

Wow. What an epiphany! Maybe not to some folks, but Corinne truly felt as if her eyes were open for the first time.

Gay people aren't bad. Gay people aren't even weird. Gay people are just...people.

"You are not wrong for loving each other. It is better to be lovers than liars." She said, hoping that Agnes could hear her.

Up and down and up and down and up and down. Corinne finally sat back. She had been kneeling for far too long. She had the sandpaper wrapped around the leg of the piano. She had the entire width of the leg encased in the sandpaper and she pulled the paper up and down repeatedly. She figured that would be the easiest and the quickest way to sand the leg.

Now exhausted, she uncurled the paper to see what it looked like.

Not bad. Not as good as she had hoped, but it really wasn't horrible. There were still some patches of green. She wondered if the paint was thicker in those spots. The wood grain was coming through, though. She was making pretty good progress all things considered.

"Okay." She huffed. She guzzled some more water. She would take a few minutes to breathe, relax, and let her legs rest before she started up again. Maybe, just maybe, she'd have this done by tonight.

Agnes took her morning stroll through the field when she saw something on the ground. She bent down to look.

It was a baby squirrel. A very young baby squirrel. Poor little critter didn't even have his fur or eyes open yet, but one of his back legs appeared broken.

"Oh you poor soul!" Agnes spoke to it. She gently scooped him up and held him in her hands until she came back into the house.

She managed her way through the kitchen. She placed a small towel on the counter and then placed him on it.

"What do you have there?" Margaret asked as entered the room.

Agnes turned and looked at her. "A baby squirrel. Poor little thing has a back leg that appears to be terribly broken."

"Oh no!" Margaret came over and looked. "Poor little creature."

"Would you mind getting the small cage out? I think that would be the best home for him."

"Of course!" Margaret ran to get the cage.

While the squirrel rested on the towel, Agnes gathered some items to create a make-shift splint for its leg. She grabbed an empty match box and folded it in half lengthwise. She grabbed some rolled gauze, and cloth-backed tape.

She came back over to the little critter. "This might hurt a bit," she whispered. "For that, I apologize. I promise you, though, this will help you to heal."

She took the folded up matchbox and held it against the bottom of its leg. Keeping the leg in a short, bent position, she took the rolled gauze and wrapped the leg and box and few times over. She then cut the gauze, grabbed the cotton-backed tape and taped it together.

The squirrel let out a tiny peep.

"Oh I know. I am so sorry, little one. I am not trying to hurt you. This will make you better, I promise."

Agnes looked back down at her little patient. "I want you to get better and stronger every day, alright?

"Once we get you all settled in your new home, I will make up a slurry for you to eat. Let's put you in there first, alright?" She picked him up and held him in the palm of her hand.

The squirrel began to relax and even rest in her hand.

"Here it is." Margaret said with the small rectangular cage.

"Splendid! Could you place that towel in there so he has something soft he can rest on?"

Margaret smiled. "Most certainly." She took the towel from the counter and placed it on the bottom of the cage.

"There you go, little man." Agnes gently said as she placed the squirrel into its new home.

They watched as the baby squirrel nestled right in with the towel.

Agnes and Margaret then looked at each other and smiled. Their newest patient was adjusting well already.

Dear Diary,

What a lovely surprise I came home to today. Margaret was playing the piano, as beautifully as always. I simply sat and was taken away into an entirely new world. A world of peace and beauty. They say music soothes the savage soul. I can only know that to be true as it soothes my soul and brings me a serenity that surpasses all others. I must say that I greatly cherish Margaret's music. It is such a wonderful gift that we can both share.

As if her music wasn't gift enough, she had prepared an absolutely divine meal. She baked a ham and served it with celery, peanuts, and she baked a pineapple upside down cake as well! It was delectable and absolutely wonderful.

What gifts she gave me! I am certainly undeserving of such kindness. She is an angel; I thank God for her daily.

Our little squirrel friend seems to be healing well. His eyes are now open to the world. His precious face always causes me to smile. He eats well and is actually quite mobile! I shall remove the splint tomorrow to see how his leg has healed.

What a splendid life we lead. It has not always been easy, but we do have much for which we are thankful. Today was a perfect example of such.

Now I shall sleep to see what wonderful gifts tomorrow has to offer.

Until then, good night.

Agnes.

Chapter Seventeen

Corinne turned on the Dremmel. It had such a high-pitched whirl. The little tip was spinning so fast, she couldn't believe it.

"Okay. Here goes nothing!" She said to herself.

She nervously placed the tip against the green molding corner of the piano. She was hardly breathing as she placed it against the wood. She winced in fear. She let it spin and whirl and work its magic.

After a few unnerving moments, Corinne pulled the tool away and stopped it. She leaned in to look.

It worked! She didn't think it would! But it did! Holy crow, the paint was gone in that corner!

Corinne laughed with excitement.

Rich's tool worked wonders! She was going to be able to finish the piano in no time! Sweet victory! Corinne was full of excitement and happiness. With great giddiness, she started it up again and really got to work.

The sun was shining brightly. The sky was a superb shade of light blue. A few thick, fluffy clouds danced around the sky. This was the perfect day, the perfect moment for this. Agnes felt a rush of emotions rise up inside her.

Her little squirrel friend looked nothing like he did when she first rescued him. His little eyes were open now; he boasted his grey fur and fluffy tail. His leg looked perfect. He healed well. He was now healthy, robust, and ready to return to the great outdoors.

Margaret came up from behind Agnes. "Are you ready?" She asked.

"Oh I am! I hope he is as well." She smiled. She bent down and placed the cage on the ground.

"Alright, little man. Your time has come. Be free!" She said gently. Agnes opened the cage door.

The baby squirrel looked around.

"It's alright, little one. Go on. Go find your family." She quietly encouraged him.

He sniffed around and hesitantly walked forward. He stopped right at the cage door. He looked around. He looked at the grass before him and sniffed it for a few moments. Finally, he stepped forward onto the ground. He took one last look around before he bounded away.

Agnes stood up and looked at Margaret; she wiped a tear from her eye.

"Another little critter saved thanks to you."

Agnes blushed. "Thank you."

"Look at him! He's doing so well. He never would have had a chance if not for you."

Agnes smiled. "Thank you, love. I'm just happy he's alright."

"Me too," Margaret smiled back. She wrapped her arm around Agnes and guided her back into the house.

The radio was playing when Agnes walked into the living room. Margaret was nowhere to be found. That was odd. Why would she have left the radio on? Where on earth could she be?

"Hello? Margaret? Are you alright?" She called out.

There were several minutes of silence.

Agnes was becoming worried. "Margaret?"

Margret leaped out from around the staircase. "Happy birthday!" She shouted.

Agnes laughed.

Margaret came into the room wearing only her slip.

"You fool!" Agnes teased. "What are you wearing?"

"It's called a slip, Agnes. It's a necessity for every woman's wardrobe." Margaret put on a strange, breathy voice.

Again Agnes laughed.

"Come here!" Margaret grabbed her by the hands and brought her into the middle of the room. She pulled her close and led her in a slow dance.

Agnes looked around.

"What are you doing?"

"Margaret, the curtains are not drawn. People can see right in! I'm sure Lacy Adams is getting an eyeful right now!"

"What if she is? This is your birthday and I love you and I want to dance with you!"

Agnes pulled back a bit.

Margaret stopped and looked squarely at Agnes. "You know, you confuse me at times."

"How so?" Agnes asked.

"You have no issue to standing up to people like Clarence. Or even that time when we watched Gone With the Wind. You were fearless. You confronted that man and not once did you flinch. You were bold and brazen. Yet, when it comes to things like this, you are petrified and fearful. You fear no man, but Lacy Adams scares the daylights out of you. I just don't understand."

Agnes looked at the floor. Margaret was right. Why was that? How was it possible for her to stand up to men in public, yet she feared dancing with her lover in the privacy of her own home? It was illogical. Not even Agnes could understand why that was.

"I'm sorry. I don't have an answer. You're right. I just..."

"Do you love me?"

"Of course I do!"

"Then dance with me. On your birthday. Come dance with me." Margaret pulled her in.

Agnes wrapped her arms tightly around Margaret, and she buried her face in Margaret's neck and shoulder. "I'm sorry," she whispered. "I love you."

Corinne flipped the page. It was hard not to smile looking back at the old photos. Pictures of her and Darryl when they were dating.

Back when they were so young and had so much life ahead of them. Back before Darryl had enlisted. Back before all the moves and emptiness. Back before she was imprisoned in this old farm house.

How she missed those days! Corinne would have given anything to go back to those days. To soak in every single moment. To grab onto Darryl and not let him leave. To walk some other path in life that wouldn't have ended here.

One lone tear escaped her eyes. Those really were the good old days, and she would never get those days back.

All she could do was pray that once Darryl was back, they could have new days that would be somewhat like that again.

She inhaled deeply and closed the photo album.

Agnes slowly strolled through the field. It was a gorgeous spring morning. It was only the beginning of April, but the sun was warm and the sky was clear. The birds were chirping; only a few clouds lightly bounced in the sky. It was the perfect morning. She happily made her way to the barn, ready to let Chief out and to do her morning barn chores. She opened the door.

Chief didn't peek his head out. It was still pretty dark in the barn, perhaps she just couldn't see him. She walked in and called his name. "Good morning, Chief! Are you ready for a new day?" Still no signs of him.

Agnes' heart dropped in fear. She walked in slowly. "Chief?" She nervously asked.

The barn was silent.

Fearing the worst, she ran to the stall door and looked in.

Chief lay on the ground, unmoving.

Agnes screamed with all her might. She ran into the stall, kneeled next to him and wept.

146

Margaret could hear Agnes' screams. She raced out of the house and ran to the barn as quickly as she could.

She stopped at the stall and saw Agnes next to Chief.

Agnes wailed as Margaret came into the stall and knelt behind her. She gently rubbed Agnes' arm. Margaret began to cry for Agnes. She could only imagine the depth of pain Agnes was feeling. Chief had been her life-long friend. The only soul that had stayed with her through childhood and adulthood. He was the only friend she had when her parents had died. He was more than just a horse. He was a soul mate of sorts.

Corinne typed in Piano repair in the search bar. Websites, pictures and videos all came up. The list was endless. What had she just gotten herself into?

She clicked on one video. Holy crow! It was twenty minutes long! She watched and listened. It didn't take long for her to become completely overwhelmed.

Okay. That might be too much. She didn't need to start off with a twenty minute one. She wanted short and simple – at least to start.

Corinne sighed heavily and looked around more. She could always bookmark all of these and go through them one at a time. She didn't need to watch them all right now, right? Besides there are so many aspects: wood repair, key repair, pedal repair, tuning, and other aspects of this restoration. This was no small undertaking. Just like with any big project, she was going to need to do this in small bits.

Okay, she was still working on fixing up the old wood and having to replace some of the panels. So she went through the list of videos on wood repair. There were four that looked promising. She bookmarked them all, and then clicked to watch the first one.

Margaret carefully placed the candelabra on top of the piano. With precision and great caution, she lit every candle.

"What are you doing?" Agnes asked. Her eyes were still bloodshot and puffy. Her face was void of any color.

Pianissimo

"Mother always taught us that when someone passes away, you are to place candles on the piano. You let them burn all the way, never blow them out. Simply let them burn until they are gone."

Agnes slowly rose out of her chair and walked over to Margaret and the piano. "What is the reason for that?"

"It is a way to honor the person who has passed; the candle light guides them to heaven. The light also shows them where we are so they can see us. It helps to keep them close - perhaps even in the house since it is on the piano."

Agnes struggled to breathe.

"The light will guide Chief to heaven, but it will also make sure that he will never be far from here."

"Thank you," Agnes' voice cracked. More tears raced down her face.

Margaret turned and gently held her.

Dear Diary,

Today has easily been the worst day of my life. Even more upsetting than when mother and father died.

It was such a beautiful morning. I thought it was going to be a lovely day. Unfortunately, I was severely mistaken.

When I went to the barn this morning, I found Chief dead in his stall. My best friend and confidant since childhood. The only soul who truly understood me. He was more than just a horse. He was my heart and soul.

Thank goodness for Margaret. God bless that woman. She has been so kind and understanding. She has listened to me wail, and she has passed no judgment on me.

She lit candles and placed them on the piano. She told me that putting candles on the piano will help to guide souls to Heaven, but will also keep them close since the piano is in the house. I've not heard of that before, but I am so grateful that she did that. She cared enough to perform a ritual which would help both Chief and I.

I don't know how I will be able to live without my beloved Chief, but I am certain that Margaret will make that life as great as it could ever be.

I don't know if I want this day to end or to never end. I loathe the idea of life going on without him. On the other hand, I just want this horrific day to be behind me, that I may never experience this pain again.

Alas, time will do what it always does: continue to press forward.

Until then, good night.

Agnes.

"Come look!" Corinne said with great excitement. Rich chuckled; he tried to keep up with her, but going down those stairs was more difficult than he thought.

He finally reached the bottom and walked over to the piano. "This is unbelievable! Every speck of green paint is gone! And look: the wood underneath looks pretty good!"

"Thanks!" Corinne replied.

"Now, have you used a really fine grit paper on it?"

"No. Should I?"

"I would." He said. "It will really smooth out the wood and peel off some of the older, thinner layers and bring out the freshest, healthiest wood."

"Really?"

"Yeah. And it will make the wood feel smooth as silk."

"Huh. I didn't know that."

"Yeah. I know it means more work for you. But at this point, you've done all the hard work. This won't be nearly as bad. I think if you just go over it a couple of time, you should be good to go."

"A couple?"

"Yes. Two, maybe three times. I gotta say, though, the wood will tell you."

"What?" Corinne asked.

"Run your hand over the wood after each time you do it. It will be soft, smooth and warm. When it feels 'right,' it will be."

"That sounds so weird."

"I know, I know. You're just going to have to trust me on this one."

"You haven't steered me wrong yet!"

Rich smiled at her. "This is going to be amazing once it's all done, Corinne. You're doing a great job and it's only going to get better from here."

"Thank you!" She smiled back.

"Okay. You sand it some more. Once it's all ready, let me know. I'll come over and we'll cut those panels and really finish it up nicely."

"Sounds like a plan. Thank you so much, Rich!"

"You are very welcome." He smiled again. "I'll talk to you soon."

Agnes steadied her feet and forced the axe down with all of her might. The log split in half beautifully.

She removed the two pieces and placed another log on the stand.

Again, she reached up and slammed the axe down. Another perfect split.

"Excuse me!" A voice called out. It was not one that Agnes recognized. It sounded like a man.

Agnes looked up.

A young man was walking towards her.

"Can I help you?" Agnes wiped the sweat off her brow.

"It is I who hopes to help you."

She looked at him intensely, and propped her foot on the block.

"Tell me why a nice lady like you is doing such hard work. Shouldn't your husband be doing this?"

Agnes laughed. "I don't have one."

The poor man's face dropped. "Oh, I am so sorry! I did not mean – I apologize for my mistake. I'm very sorry for your loss."

Agnes wondered if she should correct him or not. It would be the right thing to do, but it might make this poor man feel even more uncomfortable. She knew she needed to, though. She politely smiled. "I never married."

"Oh! Well don't I feel silly then?"

"No need. Old maids like myself are a rarity. Anyway, how can I help you?"

"My name is Ralph Masterson. I just moved here – I live right around the corner."

"Nice to meet you." Agnes shook his hand. "Welcome. I think you'll find this to be a nice little neighborhood and Louisville is a great city."

"I'm sure it is. I was wondering if you would like some help chopping your wood. I hate to see a woman having to do such brutal work."

"Well, thank you. I don't really think of it as brutal. I grew up on this farm. I was an only child, so I was working like any farmer at an early age. Then my parents passed away when I was eighteen; I have really had no choice but to be self-sufficient."

"I must say, I admire you for your strength and resiliency Miss..."

"Walker. Agnes Walker."

"Miss Walker. You're a brave and courageous soul. May I please be of assistance?"

"Actually, I am almost done for the evening. If you would like, come back on Wednesday. I'll have plenty more to be split then. And I shall make you a wonderful rhubarb pie."

Ralph smiled. "I do love a good rhubarb pie, Miss Walker."

"Rumor has it that mine is the best around here. It would be my pleasure to make one for you."

"You're a very generous lady, Miss Walker. I shall see you on Wednesday, then."

Agnes smiled brightly. "Thank you very much, Mister Masterson. See you Wednesday."

He tipped his hat to her and began to walk back in the direction from which he came.

Agnes set up another log.

"You hoo!" Lacy Adams called out to Ralph.

He stopped and looked at her.

She motioned for him to come to her.

Agnes chuckled to herself watching Lacy. She grabbed her axe and drove it right into the log.

"I saw you speaking with Miss Walker over there." Lacy said to Ralph. She was clearly trying to be discreet, but her voice was not quiet, and it carried down the street.

"I did. I offered to help her since she doesn't have a husband to chop that wood for her."

Agnes grabbed the last log and set it up.

"That's very kind of you." Lacy said. "I would caution you, though. Don't spend too much time over there. She isn't right. There's something peculiar about both of them."

"Both?" He asked.

"She has a boarder there, too. Margaret Begum. The two of them are very odd. They've been living together for years; just two women alone. I don't know what it is, but I do not like those ladies. They're just not right. Be careful if you're around them."

From where she was standing, Agnes could see Ralph was stunned. He hesitated to speak. "Okay. Thank you, Miss."

He tipped his hat to her as well and walked away.

Lacy stared at Agnes.

Agnes reached her axe into the sky and plummeted it right through the center of the log. With a loud crack, it split perfectly in half. Agnes stuck the axe on the block. She then smiled at Lacy, and walked back into the house.

Agnes slowly stepped into the barn. She had been doing this initially every day after Chief died. Now, she visited weekly.

She stopped in the doorway and inhaled. She could still smell him. She could still smell the hay and feed. There was something invigorating and addictive in the smell of a horse barn. This one even more so, because it smelled like him.

She walked over to the shelf where his curry comb rested. She held it tightly. What few hairs remained felt like angelic silk in her hands. Oh but to touch him again! What she wouldn't give to do that. This would have to suffice...for the rest of her life. This was the only way she'd ever be able to touch her beloved companion again.

The barn was so big, quiet and empty. It shouldn't be this way. It had never been this way before. The least amount of horses they ever had was the family got out of the horse trade and Chief was the only one here. He was a presence, though. Even though he was alone, this barn wasn't necessarily quiet. He was like the king here. He didn't need other horses around him. He always let the world know where he was. He ruled this barn and those fields. They were made just for him. And it was perfect. He was perfect.

This emptiness – the loss of his presence was not perfect. It was only perfectly painful. It was awful, and it shouldn't be this way.

Agnes inhaled deeply, trying to fight back the tears. Would the pain ever leave – or at least lessen? Would there ever come a day that she could accept his death and move on? Would a time come where she would not need to come in here to try to smell and feel him again? Was it possible for her to one day be complete without him? She doubted it.

She walked around. She hadn't cleaned it since he passed. There was no need to. Spider webs were plentiful in the stalls and in the walkway. There was still a fairly large pile of hay bales by the back door. What was she going to do with it? There was nothing she could do. It was getting old now, no one would want it. She was not getting another horse. So there it sat: useless and aging. Just like everything else in this barn.

Days of harsh weather had already come and gone since he died. There were more to come. There was no point in worrying about it. There was no need to fix any damage that had been done or any that would come in the future. She desperately wanted to keep the barn so she could feel connected to Chief. On the other hand, she didn't want to put in any effort into an empty barn.

Pianissimo

One last look around would have to suffice for tonight. It was getting late, and she'd best get back to the house.

"I love you. I miss you," she whispered before she left.

Chapter Eighteen

Corinne grabbed the laundry basket out of the bathroom closet. Just as she picked it up, she noticed one of the lights went out. It was odd because it faded out, it didn't pop like a bulb normally does when it goes out. But it wasn't giving off any light anymore. It must have just died strangely.

"Oh well," she thought to herself. She'd come back up and replace the bulb later.

Following her usual Sunday ritual, she cautiously brought the laundry down the very scary basement steps.

She looked over at the piano as she was loading up the washer with the first load. It was really starting to come together. It wasn't perfect, it will never be perfect. Far too much damage had incurred for it to ever be perfect again. That was alright, though. It had come a long way so far, and it was only going to get better.

She finished loading up the washer, poured her detergent and got it going.

As she came back up, Corinne noticed that a sock had fallen out. As she re-traced her steps, there were other socks, and even a pair of underwear that had fallen out of the basket. She made her way back up into the bathroom.

Without thinking she turned on the lights.

The bathroom was nice and bright.

She looked around. She couldn't find any other stray garments.

Then it struck her that the bathroom was very well lit.

Corinne looked up. Every light was on. Every light was working.

"Wait a minute." She said out loud. What the heck was going on? That one bulb had dimmed and died just a little while ago. Now it was working again! What on earth...?

She could not make sense of it at all. This house was so bizarre. Weird stuff like this seemed to be rather commonplace. Why? How? It didn't make any sense.

Corinne turned all the lights off. She waited for a minute and turned them back on. Once again, every light lit right up.

She knew she wasn't crazy. She knew she wasn't making this up. That light had stopped working. There was no question about it. It was not on earlier. She watched it stop! Now it was lighting up again. How was that possible? How on earth could that be? It wasn't even as if it could be blamed on faulty wiring. This was the first time anything like this had happened. If the wiring was bad, this would have been a constant battle.

"I give up!" She said. "I don't know what is going on with this house. I don't get it. I don't understand it at all. Who or whatever this is: I give up. You win. This stuff is just plain weird. I'm done. I am not messing around with this anymore." She put her hands up. "I give up."

Corinne turned the lights off one last time and walked out of the bathroom shaking her head.

Small tears slowly rolled down Margaret's round cheeks.

Agnes walked into the room and saw Margaret sitting, unable to move. "Margaret?" She softly asked.

Agnes came around and sat next to her. "Margaret, what's wrong?

"My father." She sniffled.

"Oh no. What happened?"

"He has pneumonia. He is in the hospital."

"Oh dear." Agnes sighed. "I am so sorry. Would you like to go see him?"

Margaret began to wail. "I don't know! I want to be with him, but I am afraid to see him in such poor condition."

Agnes gently put her arm around her. "I understand completely. You take your time. We will do whatever it is you wish. We will do whatever is best for you. Whatever you want, whatever you need."

Margaret soulfully looked at her. "God bless you." She wiped a tear away.

"Okay. The length was what again?" Rich asked.

"Fifty eight point six." Corinne said.

"Okay. Did you mark it?"

Her gaze was fixed on the wood. "Doing that right now. Give me just a second." She drew a small line at the measurement. "Done."

"Are you ready?"

She looked up at him with nervous excitement. "I guess so. Let's do it!" She smiled.

He placed the board on the miter saw, turned the saw on and sliced through the wood.

The shrill piercing sound of the saw made Corinne cringe.

The sawdust settled, and the air quieted.

Apprehensively, she looked at him.

"Well?" She asked.

"Let's see." He took the piece of mahogany wood and placed it atop the piano. "Perfect!"

It was perfect. It was an absolute perfect fit. Once it was secured, no one would have ever guessed how badly this piano had been destroyed.

She smiled with excitement. "It is!"

They both looked at it for a moment.

"You've done incredibly well. This looks great." Rich said. "But you know..."

"Oh no! Now what?"

He chuckled. "No, it's not bad. I was just going to say that it was a shame we haven't taken pictures along the way to show the progress."

"Oh! You're right! That would have been good."

He nodded in agreement.

"Well, it could be worse, I suppose." She said.

"Yeah! It could still look like it did!" He replied.

They both chortled.

"Okay," she sighed. "Let's secure this."

Rich flipped the board upside down. He began to put wood glue all along the edges.

"What is that?" Corinne asked.

"It's wood glue. I'm still going to nail it in, but this gives it a better grip all around."

"Oh, okay."

"Come on over to the other side." He said.

Corinne walked to the opposing side of the board.

"On a count of three, we're going to flip this over and position it, okay?"

"Alright."

"One...two...three!"

They both flipped the board back over and carefully placed it, making sure it was exactly where it needed to be.

"Look good?" He asked.

Corinne stepped back and looked at it carefully. "Yeah," she finally said.

He walked back and stood next to her. "Yeah! Not bad for two amateurs." He teased. "Alright. I am going to nail this in, and then we just need to wait."

"Wait?"

"Yeah. I don't want to do anything else for at least another twenty four hours. I really want to make sure this settles and has a good, strong hold before we start moving things around, adding more pieces and so on."

"Makes sense." Corinne replied.

Rich carefully hammered in nails in all four corners and in a few places along the edges.

After several long minutes of pounding, Rich made his way back to Corinne. "There you have it." He said.

She smiled up at him. "Thank you so much!"

Dear Diary,

It saddens me when the school year ends. I miss the children. Though they may aggravate me from time to time, I do genuinely care and feel almost lost without them. It just means that another chapter in my life is ending so that another may begin.

Poor Margaret's father is not doing well. It really is a shame. I don't think it shall be too long. Her sister, Josephine, has been absolutely dreadful. She is a cold and callous woman. She worries not about the death of her father, but rather of the division of his property and belongings. Can you imagine that? It's just awful, I tell you. This has put such a strain on poor Margaret, and her sister is of absolutely no use. She doesn't even help with his care, she is that far removed. I do what I can for Margaret. Although I've been down a similar path, I find it to be worse to be disappointed and hurt by a sibling's inactivity than to simply be alone.

Life is so short and unpredictable. Life can change or end in the blink of an eye. You never know what is about to happen. Yet, there is Josephine, with more concern of material objects than of her relationships with her family members. Though I wish her no harm, I do hope that changes. She needs to see – and understand – what is truly important in life.

I'd best end this here. Margaret shall be home soon, and I would like for her to have a warm dinner waiting for her arrival. Assuming God grants me another day, I shall write tomorrow.

Until then, good night.

Agnes.

"Okay," Corinne looked at the tape measurer again. "The full panel is forty three point two in height and twenty point three for the width. How do we want to do this since this one side is only missing a few inches?"

Rich walked around the piano. "Hmmm. Alright, let's do this. The other side is completely gone. Let's just start with that. We could put another piece to fill in for this side, but I'd really want to use clamps for that. I don't know if we'd be able to clamp it properly. I want time to think about that before we actually do anything."

Corinne was completely confused. "Uhhh...okay." She chuckled.

Rich laughed. "Don't worry about. We'll do the other side just like we did with the top. We'll cut it, glue it and nail it in. We'll let it sit for a couple of days and I'll figure it all out."

"Alright." She breathed heavily.

"You said it was forty three point two, right?"

"Yeah."

"Ok. Let me just mark that. Do you want to run the saw this time?"

Corinne's eyes nearly doubled in size. "What?"

"Oh come on. It's easy."

"Are you sure?"

"Sure. Come here. Let me show you."

Rich placed the piece of mahogany wood on the miter saw. "You match the line on the wood with the line marker right here. See?" He pointed to a mark on the table of the miter saw.

"Okay."

"And then you'll just pull the saw down like this." He demonstrated for her.

"You make it look too easy."

"You've done all the hard stuff already! This is easy." He waited. "Come on, I'll help you."

He smiled.

Corinne was still scared, but she decided to try anyway.

Rich held the wood so it was steady and even. "Ready?"

"I guess so."

"Go head. Pull it down!"

Corinne's heart was racing. Beads of sweat began to form on her forehead. Her hand was starting to feel shaky. She could not believe she was about to do this. She took in a deep breath, reached up and pulled the saw down. Corinne quickly closed her eyes in fear.

It seemed like an eternity hearing the saw squeal and then finally screech as it cut through the wood.

Finally there was silence. Frightened, Corinne slowly opened her eyes. "Well?"

"Look for yourself."

She looked down at the wood. It was perfectly cut. "Hey. That looks okay."

"Okay? You got it! Great job."

"Really?" Corinne's face lit up.

"Yeah! Look at it! It's perfect!"

"Wow! I really did it! And I got it right the first time!"

Rich chuckled. "You sure did. Great job."

Corinne was smiling from ear to ear. "Thanks! Thank you so much!"

"Sure. Now, let's put the glue on." He grabbed the piece and flipped it upside down. He squeezed a plentiful amount around the edges.

Together, they grabbed the board and carefully lined it up one the side of the piano Once it was perfectly set, Rich hammered some nails in.

Afterwards, they both stepped back and took a look.

"Looks pretty darn good, eh?" He said.

"It looks great!" She replied.

"It really does. You should be proud of yourself, Corinne. You've done a wonderful job." He put his arm around her. "Great job."

She looked up at him and smiled. "Thanks."

Dear Diary,

Unfortunately, Mister Begum passed away this morning. My heart is so saddened and so heavy for Margaret. It is a terrible loss. She has all of my sympathy.

Her sister continues to be a monster. We were all gathered together: Josephine and Timothy, Walter and Ruth, Margaret and myself. Josephine did not even look at me, let alone address me. Nor did she with her own sister.

The family reminisced, as anyone would. There was also talk of the funeral services and such. Not once did Josephine ask Margaret what her thoughts or opinions were. Walter included her occasionally, but not too often. It was as if neither of us was there; that we were simply on the outside looking in and eavesdropping on a private conversation.

After we came home, poor Margaret wept. It was tragic to see. I held her and comforted her as best I could.

Margaret told me that she was more pained by being ostracized by her own siblings than by anything else. Their lack of compassion or consideration devastated her tremendously. She asked me why might they be so callous. I had no answers.

What is wrong with us that we are so disliked? Are we truly unnatural and ungodly women? Neither of means to bring any harm to anyone else. Yet we are treated so maliciously. I wonder if there are others in the world like us. I would like to think that there are. It's so difficult to discern for certain, though. For if there are, I am sure they need to be as secretive as we. It's rather tragic that we do have to live this way. I certainly do not enjoy being watched nor being overly cautious. I must admit that I loathe the clandestineness and privacy. I also hate to admit that I greatly fear what could happen if anyone were to truly discover the nature of our relationship.

I wish I understood this better. To know whether or not we are unnatural or ungodly. To be able to understand and explain our level of commitment to each other. To not be so hated and disregarded.

Perhaps one day, all of this will come to light. Hopefully the future will bring more people like us, but people who are braver than we. I can only pray for a day when people like us are able to live normal lives and not be so closely monitored. Should that day come, even if I am in Heaven, I will rejoice in knowing that there is nothing inherently wrong with either Margaret or myself.

Poor Margaret is sobbing again. I'd best go tend to her. I shall write again tomorrow, as I always do.

Until then, good night.

Agnes.

"Alright. There you go. It's all set." Rich said.

"Wow! I can't believe it's done. Well, mostly done, anyway."

"You took on one hell of a project."

"You're not kidding. There were many times I wondered what I had gotten myself into."

"Oh I'll bet. This wasn't just small repairs here and there. This was a big project."

"Uh huh!" She agreed.

"Now," he started.

"Oh no!"

"It's not terrible. But," he continued. "You should probably sand it one more time."

"What?!" She exclaimed.

"I want you wait till everything has bonded, and the filler has dried before you do it anyway. But one quick, light sanding with a fine grit paper to make sure all the wood is smooth and even all over – nail holes, the old pieces and the new boards. This way you won't have inconsistencies in texture and color once you finish it with polyurethane."

Corinne took in a deep breath. "Okay."

"Like I said, wait a couple of days anyway. Then lightly sand it. Use a cloth to remove all of the dust and then use the poly. Got it?"

She looked up at him. "Got it. I did learn from the best, you know."

Rich laughed. "I don't know about that. I just want you to be happy and proud of all your hard work."

"I really could not have done this without you. It's our work, and I am very grateful for everything you've done."

"No problem. I'm gonna get going. I don't want to miss Susie's dinner tonight. She's making spaghetti and meatballs."

"Nice! Enjoy."

"What about you?" Rich asked.

"I'll probably just have a frozen dinner."

"Do you want to come over? She makes great spaghetti."

"No, it's fine. Thank you. You've done enough for me. Plus I need to rest up since I have to sand this beast. Again!" She chuckled.

"Alright. You be good."

"I will, Rich. Thanks again!"

"Margaret!" Agnes called from the other bedroom. "Come see what I just found!"

Margaret walked in from the living room.

Agnes stood proudly in the closet door frame holding up a pair of black trousers.

"What...?"

"They're pants! These are my father's trousers!" She looked down at them. "I can't believe they're here. I had no idea. I thought all of his belongings were long gone."

"What do you intend to do with them?"

"Well I think I should wear them!"

"What?" Margaret laughed.

Agnes pulled the pants on under her dress.

Margaret laughed hysterically. "Now that, my love, is quite the fashion!"

"I agree. It is all the rage in Paris!"

"I could only imagine." Margaret chuckled.

Agnes began walking around the room. "I must say, I do quite like this."

"You do?"

"It would be better with just a blouse rather than this dress. This is comfortable, though." She sat in the chair. She sat with her legs open and she leaned back in the chair. "So this is what it feels like to be a man! Oh this is so much better than having to act like a dreadful lady. You may sit anyway you choose. You may slouch. You need not worry about posture or appearing inappropriate. Oh this is wonderful! You should try it, Margaret. I think you shall enjoy this as much as I."

Margaret chuckled again. "I'm not quite so sure of that. I think I shall leave you to be the man. I am quite comfortable as I am."

Agnes quickly pulled the pants off, bundled them up and tossed them at Margaret. "Spoil sport!" She teased.

Margaret leaned back in laughter. "Oh you are too much!"

"Shall we keep them, then? You may parade around the house as Michael, not Margaret."

Again Margaret burst into laughter. "Oh sweet Agnes! This is why I love you so! Only you could make me laugh like this."

Agnes walked over and kissed Margaret on the forehead. "And this is why I love you so. You laugh at my silly humor and you understand me like no one else can."

Margaret looked up and smiled at her. "We truly are two of a kind."

"Indeed. We are perfect together." Agnes smiled back.

Dear Diary,

Today was brimming with news. We – or at least I – felt inundated with change.

Pianissimo

First, the day brought us an unusual situation. Nathaniel Adams, Lacy's husband, came over. He apologized for his wife's behavior. Multiple times, actually. He seemed so genuinely embarrassed, saddened and apologetic. They clearly had a difference of opinion about us.

He called on us to see if Margaret would be willing to let bygones be bygones and to teach their children, Richard and Abigail, how to play the piano.

Margaret, being the wonderful woman that she is, was more than happy to provide lessons for them.

He was so appreciative of her kindness. He's a good man. How he ended up with such a hag as herself, I do not know or understand. It's wrong and hateful of me to say such things, I know. Our conversation today has really changed my perspective on their family, and on her.

Regardless, he is a good man, and Margaret will gladly educate his children. Perhaps this will change Lacy. Even more hopefully, this could possibly bridge a friendship between her and us.

In other news, the war has finally come to an end. A second world war. How tragic that our world has turned into this. Dictators killing people. Countries attacking and controlling other countries. Hatred, fear, propaganda, massacre. Sad, so tragic and sad. All I can do is shake my head, for I can't even fully understand how things have come to this.

What changes – both good and bad – we have experienced in our lifetimes. Two world wars. Airplanes and automobiles becoming common household and commonly used items. Technological changes like radios and moving pictures. Prohibition. From the Roaring Twenties to the Great Depression. We have seen it all.

Truth be told, I worry about the future. We have watched such horrible and brutal acts like those of Hitler and Stalin. If our world today can create such monsters, what else lies ahead?

I'm quite happy the war is over. It is nice to be able to breathe and not worry about friends and loved ones who must see the atrocities of war. One less thing to fret about, I suppose. I pray that this peace is one that lasts not just for decades, but for centuries. May this bring the end of such death, anger, and evil.

Thankfully, the news of the day was all good. It was different, but all so wonderfully positive. I suppose all of this news proves that every day does prove to be an adventure. With that thought, I shall retire and see what tomorrow will bring.

Until then, good night.

Agnes.

Holy crow! There were way too many brands of stain, finishes, and colors. It was overwhelming. Corinne looked at can after can. She didn't know what she wanted. What would look good on Mahogany? Would a gloss finish be too much on a piano? Was a matte finish too dull? What about the colors? Would any of them turn the wood into some God-awful orange color or something? Corinne stood completely dumbstruck in front of all the cans of polyurethane.

"Can I help you miss?" A young man came up on her left.

"I sure hope so!" She replied pathetically.

He smiled. "What are you looking for?"

"Polyurethane. For mahogany wood."

"Is it a table? A buffet?"

She wrinkled her nose. "A piano."

His eyes lit up. "A piano? Cool!"

Corinne smiled. "Thanks." She briefly paused. "So I don't know what color to go with or if I should use a gloss finish or not."

"A piano is something that stands out. It's not something that you want to look dull or dirty."

"Okay."

"I would go with at least a semi-gloss. If you're worried about too much shine, semi is your best way to go. It gives the piano a nice finished look, but it won't be overly shiny."

Wow. This guy really knew his stuff. And he was interested in what she was doing! He was listening and giving her tips, not just rambling off any stupid, random information. Corinne was impressed. "Okay, so we'll do a semi-gloss. But what about color?"

"That depends on you. Do you really want to color the wood with a stain or are you looking to just bring out the natural grain and highlights of the wood?"

Corinne had to think. She didn't know. She didn't expect this to be so involved. She really wasn't sure. "I don't know."

"Okay. Let me show you some things." He motioned for her to follow.

They walked down the aisle to some wood swatches.

"Take a look at these. You can see which ones are stains and which ones are finishes."

Corinne flipped through the different pieces. She was becoming even more confused! "Oh boy! I don't know!"

"Would you like my opinion?" The young guy asked.

"Yes, please!"

"I would tell you to use a finish, not a stain. Personally, I like the natural look of wood. I like bringing out the natural color and grain. Don't get me wrong, some stains are great. I guess it's kind of what you're looking to do with this piano."

Corinne chuckled. "You up for a long story?"

"Sure!"

"Long story short, it's a restoration. It was in the basement of my house when I first moved in. It was painted an awful olive green color. It was missing pieces; it was in terrible condition. I decided to fix it up. It's been a very long and difficult process. It will never be original, but it's from 1907 and now it looks like a nice, antique piano."

"Then I would definitely just use a clear finish. If you've had to work that hard, you want that thing to stand out. You don't want it to look dull or fake or just...not right. A nice finish will brighten up the wood, bring out the grain and make it look like it should."

He pulled a can off the shelf and placed it by her feet. "You'll want to do one nice thick, even coat first. Then wait twenty four to forty eight hours and do a second coat. The wood – especially the older wood – is really going to suck up that first layer. So that's why you want to make it thick. You want to drench the wood in it. The second coat will go on nice and smooth and it will dry in no time. That'll give it that really polished, finished look."

Corinne smiled. What a great, nice, helpful kid this was! She still couldn't get over how much thought he put into all of this.

"Sounds like a plan. I can't tell you how much I appreciate all your time and help. You really went above and beyond. Thank you!"

"I think it's really cool that you did that. I'm glad I was able to help you."

"When it's all done, I should show you a picture."

"That would be awesome!" His eyes sparkled. "I would love that! It would be so cool! Thanks!"

"You bet!" Corinne smiled back. "Next time you see me, I'll be in here with a picture for you."

"Cool!" He exclaimed.

"What was your name?"

"Kevin."

"Okay Kevin. I'll ask for you. I'll bring you a picture soon!" Corinne smiled one last time before picking up the can of polyurethane and walking up to the check-out line.

Agnes walked into the living room. "Hello, my love."

Margaret wearily looked up at her.

Agnes leaned down. "Are you alright?"

Margaret sighed. "Yes. I am exhausted."

"Oh Margaret. Go upstairs. Get some rest. You need not stay up."

Margaret smiled weakly. "Agnes, I know I should. I miss you, though. We have had such limited time together as of late. I miss your company. Every moment together is a gift to me. As much as I would like to sleep, I would also like to be by your side."

Agnes smiled brightly at her. "My beautiful darling. Come upstairs. I will join you. Better yet, I shall lay next to you and I will read."

Margaret's eyes lit up. "You will? What shall you read?"

Agnes' smile grew larger. "Whatever the lady requests."

"Oh Agnes, you are so wonderful to me. Thank you."

"It is my pleasure. Now, do you care to join me?"

"Indeed!" Margaret stood up, hooked her arm into Agnes', and the couple went upstairs.

My Dearest Margaret,

Yet another year has come and gone. Another year of beauty and tears. We have had some amazing moments and some terrible moments.

Even at the very worst days that life has given us, I could not have asked to have a better person by my side.

You have always comforted and consoled me. You have loved and accepted me even when I was not deserving.

I don't know how you are always able to be such a bright and beautiful soul. There is not one blemish I could ever find in you. You are joyous, compassionate, considerate, selfless, giving, wonderful and simply amazing.

Happy anniversary, my love. You are a truly wonderful woman. I thank God for you daily. You have my heart now and forever.

I love you with all of my heart and soul,

Agnes.

The thick autumnal clouds sat in the sky as if it were a table. The bottoms of the clouds appeared flat and they fluffed upwards in all various shades of blue and grey. The crisp golden and red leaves of the trees swayed gently in the breeze. The light, distinct scent of fresh, ripe apples floated through the air. A few areas of the old red barn peeked through the thick, lush ivy that had overtaken the poor old building. The ancient roof sagged down under the weight of years gone by. It was both beautiful and wretched.

Agnes looked around. She looked behind them, towards Lacy Adams' house. She couldn't be sure if she could actually see anyone, or not. She focused her eyes. She thought she might have seen a shadow in the window. Perhaps not. It was too difficult to be certain. Regardless, Agnes was certain they were watching.

Margaret kept her arm around Agnes. "Relax. No one can see us. Just look." She gently coaxed.

Agnes turned and beheld the view. The view of the red barn contrasting against the grey sky and dark green ivy. The view of the light green fields that expanded behind the barn. The sight of where she and Chief used to simply run – where she was truly free. Where she worked as a child and absorbed the sun's rays year round. A view that was a sight she knew better than the sight of her own face. The sight of her childhood.

"You know it won't be long," Margaret spoke quietly.

"I know." Agnes' lip began to quiver. Knowing that the barn that used to house her beloved Chief was crumbling caused her to crumble. "Sadly, it's all I have left of him."

"It's just a representation of him, love. You still have him. You have your memories, we still have the fields. He will always be with you, always be a part of you. Nothing can ever take that away from you. Years, decades, and perhaps even centuries from now, when this barn and this house are long gone, you will still share your bond with him. It will never be gone – not now, not ever."

Tears quietly streamed down Agnes' cheeks as the two stood in silence, absorbing the view before it was gone permanently.

Corinne hooked up her camera to her computer. It took a moment for the pictures to upload. She took a sip of her lemonade while she waited.

There! Fifteen pictures uploaded. She hoped at least one of them came out okay. She began to scroll through.

It was hard. The lighting down there was so terrible, and her camera was just a cheap, junky one, so the flash wasn't that great anyway. Some of the pictures were okay; most were very shadowy.

Then she clicked on picture twelve. That was it! That shot was perfect. The lighting was good, the shadows were minimal. The piano glistened in what little light there was. It looked shiny and new. It looked amazing. Corinne was really proud of herself. She was proud of the work and effort she put into that piano, and proud of taking such a great picture.

She smiled at herself. That was really pretty good. There might be something to all of this after all. Not only did she reignite her love of music, she branched out and made a friend in Rich, and she did something she's never done before. She learned new things and gained appreciation for things she had never imagined possible.

"Not bad," she whispered to herself.

She clicked on the print icon, and waited for the printer to spit out a nice copy of the picture.

She grabbed the photo and got into her car. Corinne quickly drove down to the hardware store.

Once inside, she walked right over to the customer service. "Hi."

"Hello ma'am. How can I help you?"

"I was wondering if Kevin was working today."

"Kevin please come to the customer service desk." She paged him.

"Oh okay!" Corinne was slightly surprised. That was a rather rapid and unusual way to answer her question.

After just a moment or two, Kevin made his way over to the desk.

"Kevin, this lady would like to speak with you." The girl said.

A look of fear came over him.

"Oh! No, it's okay. It's good!" Corinne reassured him.

"Hey, wait a minute. Aren't you the woman with the piano?"

Corinne smiled and nodded. "I wanted to show you this." She handed him the printed out picture.

"That's the piano?" He asked with great excitement.

"Yeah. That's the piano after the two coats of polyurethane, just like you told me."

"That is incredible! That looks so good! That's so cool!"

Corinne laughed at his enthusiasm.

"No, really! I never could have imagined it looked anything like this based on what you told me. This looks great! And look at that shine! Are you happy you went with the clear semi-gloss?"

"Oh absolutely! I think that was the perfect choice. Thank you!"

Kevin smiled at her. "No problem." He handed her back the sheet. "Thanks for bringing this in."

"No, no, no. This is for you to keep. I printed this out for you. It's yours, if you want it."

His eyes lit up. "Really?"

Corinne chuckled. "Yes, really."

"That's awesome! That is so cool! Thank you so much!"

"You are very welcome, Kevin. Thanks for all your help. Take care." Corinne flashed one last smile before heading back out to her car.

Dear Diary,

The barn has finally collapsed. It is such a painful sight. Now every little remnant I had of him is gone. It's all gone. I have nothing left. No images, no stable, no old curry combs laying on the barren shelves in the barn. It is now all just a pile of rubble. For years since he left me, the sight of the barn was the only thing that would bring me any kind of solace. Now I have nothing to see, nothing that I could possibly hold on to. What a cavernous hole I have in my heart from all of this. This is a devastating pain.

The view from the back of the house does not look normal without the sight of the barn. Now all I have is a giant pile of wood and stone. Tell me, what am I to do with that? Do I burn it, causing myself more anguish? Do I leave it there to rot and disappear, and to pain myself further by knowing what that rubble once was? There is absolutely no resolution that would be easy or painless.

How I hate this. I feel so broken and empty without my Chief, and especially now without his barn. Perhaps this sounds foolish, I don't know. Do many women weep over the loss of their horse? Do many women bond with their horses such as I with him? Do others consider their horses to be more of a companion than a work animal? Does anyone consider all animals to be little souls as I do? Probably not. I must sound like a foolish school girl.

Pianissimo

I might be a foolish school girl, but that does not take away my sadness. My broken hart is anything but fictional. The pain is quite tremendous.

I suppose I should try to get some rest. I still have to go teach in the morning despite my sorrow. Hopefully tomorrow's sunshine will ease the pain in my heart, even if only a small portion.

Until then, good night.

Agnes.

Chapter Nineteen

Agnes gathered her belongings and waited for Margaret.

"Excuse me, Miss Walker?" A strange voice came from the doorway.

Agnes looked up. A dapper young man with bright blonde hair wearing a striking blue suit stood in the doorway watching her.

"Can I help you, young man?" She asked.

"Miss Walker, it's me. David Butler."

Agnes' jaw dropped. The small, shy young boy had somehow transformed into a handsome young man. "David?" She asked in shock. "Is it really you?"

He flashed a smile. "Yes, Miss Walker. It's David Butler."

"Oh!" She exclaimed. She ran over to him and hugged him. "Look at you! What a handsome young man! I cannot believe it's been that many years that you have transformed this way."

"The years have gone by quickly."

She smiled. "Indeed they have! Come in. Have a seat. Tell me what you're doing with your life."

He walked behind her back into the classroom. "Well, ever since having you as a teacher, I have worked hard and studied diligently."

"I am so proud." She beamed with joy.

Margaret stopped in the doorway. She saw them talking. She stepped aside and waited in the hall, on the other side of the wall.

"I wanted to see you so I could speak to you personally." David said.

"What about?"

"There is something that I would like to tell you."

Agnes looked at him with confusion in her eyes.

"I am leaving soon."

"You are? Where are you going?"

"I was accepted into a wonderful university."

Her eyes lit up. "You did? Where are you going? What will you study?"

His smile grew. "I'm going to Harvard, Miss Walker."

She was stunned. She could hardly breathe. "You will be attending Harvard University?"

"Yes ma'am. I have you to thank. Had you not taken the time to help me and work with me, I would never have been able to do this."

"David, I'm just in shock. I am so happy for you. I am incredibly proud of you. Now tell me, what will you study there?"

His brown eyes beamed. "Literature."

Agnes couldn't help but chuckle. "Literature?"

"Yes! When you taught me, you spoke to me, you asked me questions and encouraged me to think and interpret literature. I will never forget that. You turned on a light switch for me. You taught me to look at things with different eyes. You taught me not to simply read, but to understand. You ignited a passion in me for literature. Now, I cannot imagine my life without it. You have given me a purpose and a passion in life."

A few small tears quietly rolled down Agnes' cheeks. "I am in awe of you, David. You are such an inspiration. You are living proof that if a person is determined enough and applies themselves, they can do anything. You are a hero."

He smiled and his cheeks blushed a bit. "Thank you, Miss Walker. You are my hero."

"Oh David!" She embraced him again. "I am so incredibly proud of you. Promise me you'll stay in touch."

"Oh I will, Miss Walker! You are my favorite teacher. I will never forget you, and I shall write you often."

"That would be splendid. Thank you, David." She gave him one final hug. "I wish you all the best in your endeavors. You will succeed and do well. I have no doubt about that!" She smiled up at him.

"Thank you, Miss Walker. Thank you for everything you have done for me. May God bless you!" He smiled, and slowly left the room.

Margaret waited a few moments before peering her head inside the room. "Who was that?" She asked softly.

"You'll never believe it in a hundred years."

"Do tell!"

"That was David Butler."

Margaret gasped. "It was?"

"Yes!"

"He's such a handsome young man! He looks like he's doing well for himself."

"Very much so!" Agnes exclaimed. "He is leaving to go off to university."

"Really? Where will he study?"

"Harvard!"

"Harvard University?" Margaret asked in shock.

"Indeed! And you'll never believe what his studies will be!"

"What?"

"Literature!"

"Oh, you must be joking."

"No, Margaret! I couldn't believe it either. He said that when I taught him, I opened his eyes to literature and helped him to interpret and understand it. He said I ignited an unknown passion within him and he could not imagine his life without literature."

Margaret beamed looking at Agnes. "I've always said you're an amazing woman. Look at what you have done! Look at how you have touched that young man, and changed his life!"

"I am...flabbergasted. I am so proud of him."

"As you should be. Don't discredit yourself, though. You gave him something that no one else could: kindness and patience. His future is what it is on account of your assistance."

"Margaret," Agnes sighed. "Have you ever wondered if our work has ever really mattered?"

"I have. I have often wondered if we were actually reaching our students or not. Especially in the days of Clarence Harrison. Days when we were examined and questioned and hated. Days that seemed to have no brightness to them. Those days are behind us, Agnes. Even in those dark days, you still surmounted his bigotry and created something good in the life of a child."

More tears began to flow from Agnes' crystal blue eyes. "He told me he would never forget me and he said, 'may God bless you.'" She stopped and leaned in closely to Margaret's ear. "Those were the finest words I have ever heard since you declared your love to me all those years ago." She whispered.

Margaret stepped back and smiled. "Good. You deserved them."

"Thank you." She smiled back. "What an amazing day!"

"Indeed! Are you ready to go home?"

Agnes paused and wiped away her tears. "I suppose I am. I might just skip all the way home, though."

Margaret laughed. "I should love to see an old lady skipping down the street!"

Agnes jokingly narrowed her eyes. "I am sorry to inform you that you won't get to see that today as I am not an old lady!" She winked at Margaret before grabbing her purse. "Let's go home. Let us celebrate this wonderful day."

As they had done before so many days, and for so many years, they walked home arm in arm.

Margaret stopped playing to cough. She must be coming down with a terrible cold. She coughed and coughed. After a few moments, she thought she could resume again. She played only a few keys when the need to cough consumed her yet again.

Agnes came from around the staircase. "Margaret, are you alright?"

Margaret cleared her throat one last time. "I am," her voice cracked. "I do believe I am coming down with a rather nasty cold."

"It certainly sounds like it. Let me make you some tea with honey."

"Oh! That would be delightful. Thank you."

Agnes placed her hand on Margaret's shoulder. She smiled when she looked down at her. "But of course. Anything for you, my love."

Agnes could hear Margaret continuing to cough while she made the tea. This was dreadful. She hoped it wouldn't be anything too serious.

After a few minutes, Agnes reappeared with Margaret's tea.

"Thank you." Margaret choked. She took several small sips. "Oh, this is perfect. It is working wonders already!"

"Good! I'm glad to hear it." Agnes paused. "Will you be going in today?"

"I had no plans to stay home." Margaret took another sip of her tea.

"Are you feeling well enough to teach?"

"I think so. I don't feel ill; it's just a bad cough."

"Alright. Please be careful, though."

"I will." Margaret smiled up at Agnes.

Both women sat around the radio. The music indicated their favorite story was about to start.

Agnes placed her hand on Margaret's knee.

Margaret smiled in return.

Just as the story began, Margaret began coughing. She quickly got out of her chair and ran to cough in the kitchen, so as not to disturb Agnes.

She was coughing for several minutes. She tried desperately to remain quiet.

Agnes walked in.

Margaret waved her hand. "No." She hacked. "Don't worry about me. Go listen to the show."

Agnes came closer. "Margaret, I am not going to leave you here coughing endlessly while I selfishly listen to a radio show. I'm worried about you." She waited for a moment. "This isn't right. It's not normal. I'm worried about you. This has been doing on for weeks now."

Margaret finished another cough. "Yes," she cleared her throat. "You know how it is, though. Some coughs just linger."

Agnes looked her. Her expression was forlorn. "Margaret, dear. I fear this is more than that. You need to be seen by a doctor."

Margaret coughed a few times more. "Alright." She acquiesced. "We shall call Doctor Clarke in the morning."

Agnes nodded her head in approval. "Good." She walked over to the cupboards. "Would you like me to make some more tea with honey for you?"

"I would love that. Thank you."

Agnes waited nervously in the waiting room. How she hated not being able to accompany Margaret. She hoped and prayed with each passing moment that Margaret would come out and they could return home.

"Excuse me, Miss Walker?" Doctor Clarke called out from the entrance to the exam rooms.

"Yes?" Agnes stood up with both hope and trepidation.

"Please come with me. There is something we need to discuss."

Agnes' stomach dropped. She felt ill and weak. She didn't know if she could walk over to him. Small step by small, tiny step, she came over to the doctor.

"Miss Walker," he said quietly. "Unfortunately your friend has Tuberculosis. Her case is rather severe. We need to get her to the hospital. Will you be able to inform her family so that they may be able to visit and make any important decisions if necessary?"

Agnes fought with all her might to keep the tears away. She was merely a friend. Margaret's family now took priority over her.

No one, especially this doctor, could have any inkling as to how deeply Agnes was hurting right now. Each breath was a battle. She wanted to cry, scream, hit the wall, fall to the floor. She wanted the world to know that she needed to be with Margaret, not them. What a horrific moment this was.

Her voice was scratchy. "Certainly."

"Alright then." He smiled. "You go home and get some rest. Miss Begum will receive the best care possible, and she won't be alone since her family will be there." He started to turn away, but stopped himself. "Thank you for bringing her in today. You're a good friend." He turned and walked away.

Agnes held her breath until she went outside. She dashed to the car and wept. Agnes let her guard down. She cried uncontrollably. She wailed from the pit of her soul. This was a pain that surpassed all others. Hers was a sadness that was too great for words.

She had no idea how much time passed, her grief was all consuming. She knew at some point, she would have to manage the drive home. Even worse, she would need to call Josephine and Walter.

Agnes held Margaret's hand. Her grip was weak, and slightly cold.

"Please don't give up on me," Agnes whispered. "Please get better so you can come home with me."

"I am trying. I will never give up on you." Margaret's scratchy voice replied.

A nurse walked in. "Alright Miss Walker, visiting hours are over."

Agnes looked up at her with pain in her eyes. "Please, may I stay?"

"Only family members are allowed to stay with patients beyond visiting hours."

"Look! Where is her family? Nowhere! They are nowhere to be found. They have not come yet once. Day in and day out poor Margaret has stayed here and neither her brother nor sister has come to visit. They are not here and they are not coming. Please let me stay in their stead."

"I'm sorry, Miss Walker. I cannot let you. You should probably go home and get some rest. It sounds like you need some. You can come back in the morning and visit Miss Begum again."

Agnes stared up at her. She knew this nurse was simply following the rules, but how she detested the rules.

"Alright. I shall come back in the morning." She submitted. Agnes looked back at Margaret. "Stay strong. I will see you again first thing tomorrow morning, alright?"

"Alright." Margaret smiled weakly. "You are my dearest friend and I love you for it."

Agnes smiled through the tears that had just begun to flow from her eyes. "You are my dearest friend. We've known each other for many years. You are a good woman, and I love you too."

Agnes reluctantly release Margaret's hand.

"Until tomorrow." She whispered before she slowly exited Margaret's room.

Margaret was pale and weak. She looked frail.

"How are you doing, my love?" Agnes asked gently.

"I suppose I'm alright. This is just very difficult." Even her voice was weak.

"I know. Please stay strong. You can fight this. Once you're all better, you can come home with me." One solitary tear raced down Agnes' face.

"Oh I would love that dearly." Margaret coughed. The cough was only getting worse. It was longer and deeper; it sounded horrendous.

"Please stay brave and strong. Keep fighting. You can overcome this."

"I will overcome this." Margaret struggled to smile.

Agnes smiled back weakly. "That's my girl. Keep getting rest and keep getting better."

"I shall."

The nurse hadn't come in yet. Visiting hours were coming to a close, so it was only a matter of moments before they would be separated yet again.

Agnes took the opportunity to quickly and gently kiss Margaret's hand.

As soon as she placed her hand back on the bed, the nurse came.

"Alright ladies."

Agnes began to stand.

"No." Margaret hacked. "Please let her stay tonight. She has been here with me every day, and has been asked to leave every night. No one in my family has come to visit once in all the time I've been here. Please, please let her stay."

"Only next of kin, in case something were to happen, Miss Begum. I'm sorry, but Miss Walker is not your next of kin. She cannot stay.

Agnes and Margaret looked at each other.

Agnes took in a deep breath. "It's alright," she tried to comfort Margaret. "I will be back in the morning just as I have always been."

She stood up and nodded to the nurse. Agnes then turned her attention back to Margaret. "Get some good rest so that you may feel better tomorrow. Pleasant dreams."

Margaret fought to smile one last smile before Agnes left.

Agnes walked into the hospital as she had every day for the past few weeks. She walked towards Margaret's room when one of the nurses stopped her.

"Miss Walker?"

"Yes?" Agnes answered with great angst in her voice.

"Miss Walker, I'm sorry to tell you this, but Miss Begum passed away this morning at around 6:30."

"She's...gone?" Agnes' lip quivered and tears freely flowed from her blue eyes.

"Yes, ma'am. I'm sorry. We contacted her next of kin. I told them that they might want to call you to inform you, but I see they haven't."

"No, not at all." Agnes tripped over her own words. "This is the first I've heard of it." She tried to breathe. "Tell me, did Walter or Josephine every come to visit her?"

The nurse fidgeted and shifted her weight. She appeared uneasy. "No. Josephine did come down to identify the body, but she left immediately after that."

"So Margaret's own family refused to see her at any point during all this time and poor Margaret had to die alone?"

The nurse stood looking at Agnes. "I...I'm sorry, Miss Walker."

"I know you are. I know this is nothing you did. It just breaks my heart that she died alone." What little composure Agnes had left was now gone as she deeply grieved. "What kind of family doesn't visit their own sister as she's dying? What kind of people are they?"

The nurse reached out and gently rubbed Agnes' arm.

After several weak, sobbing breaths, Agnes looked back at the nurse. "I am so sorry. You should not have had to see me like this." She again tried to breathe deeply. "May I see her? May I visit her one last time?"

"Unfortunately no. I am so sorry, Miss Walker, but they have already taken her to prepare her for the services.

Agnes choked on her tears. "I see. Well thank you very much for the information." Agnes cleared her throat and walked out of the hospital fighting back even more tears.

My Dearest Margaret,

You left me today. Yours was a long, dreadful struggle. You fought valiantly, my love. Unfortunately the tuberculosis won.

I cannot tell you how deeply I grieve right now. There is such a hole in my heart. My life is empty and meaningless without you. It's been hours and they have been tortuous at best.

I was not allowed to be with you. That is the worst part. Being separated from you. I lost you before you even passed. That ignites such an anger and a pain within that I am actually fearful of how I feel.

I cannot believe you are gone. You have been with me for so many years. You were always present in my life. Even if we weren't together during the day, I could come home with joy knowing you were there waiting for me.

I will be coming home to an empty house. Chief will not be there. Neither will you. I don't even have any little patients right now. I am in complete isolation.

Breathing is incredibly painful. I don't want to breathe without you. I hate that my heart continues to beat. Why? I have lost everything and everyone who has ever had any significance in my life. What on earth could be left that I must continue to live?

Margaret, I don't think I have ever properly told you how I feel. Of course I wait until you have passed. Aren't we supposed to tell our loved ones how we feel while they still live so they can pass knowing they were loved?

Every breath, every moment, every heartbeat of mine were all for you. There was not any facet of my life and being that wasn't completely dedicated to you. You, your joy, and your happiness were my only concerns in life.

Did you know that every morning, I would come down the stairs and simply listen to you play? Your music was heavenly! It was such a wonderful way to start each new day. I treasure those moments and memories so deeply – far greater than any words could ever possibly try to describe.

How am I to carry on without you? There is nothing left for me here. Each moment that passes without your presences kills my soul. I have only feared one thing in my life and that was living without you. This is my greatest fear realized. I don't know how I will manage. I don't think I'll be able to manage without you.

Did you know that the sun rises and sets for you? That the moon waxes and wanes solely for you? That the stars shine for your eyes only? That I live and love for you only?

Margaret, you are my life and my love. You took my heart with you when you went to heaven.

Please tell me about Heaven. More importantly, please wait for me there.

Pianissimo

I don't want to end this letter. I don't want to end this love. I don't want to end this life.

Margaret, dear, sweet, beautiful, wonderful, perfect Margaret. How deeply and greatly I miss you already. Please come back to me.

I love you with all of my heart and soul,

Agnes.

Dear Diary,

My beloved Margaret has passed on. The tuberculosis won early this morning.

It was so horrible watching her suffer. She was in such pain and distress, and I was completely unable to help her. What kind of person am I? There must have been something I could have done to have helped her.

I pray she is at peace now. All I can do is pray that she has found comfort and love. She is with Chief, our parents, and predecessors. Hopefully they are all restored and healthy and joyful. I know that the angels will always pale in comparison to the beauty of her soul. I do hope that everyone can see her for the precious gem she is.

I lit candles and placed them on her piano. I pray their light is guiding her to Heaven this very moment, while keeping her close to her beloved piano and to me.

She is such a God-send. I cannot imagine living without her. She gave me joy, love, compassion, devotion, and purpose. She has always been the center of my world. Life without her is truly meaningless.

I don't know what to do with myself. I am overcome with emotions and memories.

I was very saddened by the deaths of my parents. I was devastated by the death of Chief. Now I have lost all hope with the passing of my beloved.

No one can ever love as I have loved her. No one will ever truly understand the depth of our connection. There is not one soul on this earth who can ever comprehend the life and love we shared. No one will ever have such devotion as I have had for her.

Ours surpasses all love stories across time. There will never be a love as great as ours.

I am at a loss for words, and yet my mind is riddled with words, thoughts, feelings, and memories. I should like this day to close, but I know sleep will elude me.

I suppose my lot in life was that I was to be alone. To live without parents, without companions, without my beloved.

I am reading my words and I am in shock. There seems to be no fluidity. My thoughts are jumbled. There is no line of logic. Just random thoughts and emotions. I suppose that is to be expected at a time like this.

I don't know what else to say or what I am to do with myself.

I suppose I shall write another time. I shall go watch the candles burn on the piano.

Until then, good night.

Agnes.

Agnes stood in the dark, her arm rested heavily on the piano. The moonlight slithered its way in through the window, shadowing her tall, lean figure on the wall. Agnes couldn't move. Even if she could, she wouldn't want to. The silence pierced her soul. The room sat mute, but how the sounds of even just a few days previous flooded her mind.

Unable to breathe, unable to move, she stayed motionless; the piano was the only thing supporting her.

Chapter Twenty

"It really is a shame about Margaret. Especially since she never married nor had any children. What has she left us? Nothing. She was a beautiful woman. She would have made an excellent wife and mother. Why she chose a life of solitude, I'll never understand." Josephine said as they all proceeded in the house. "Alas, that is the life that my sister chose."

She walked past the piano and noticed the burning candles Agnes had placed on it.

"You believe that silly hog wash?" Josephine asked Agnes.

"It was what she told me."

"Indeed. She claims mother taught her that, though I don't remember mother ever saying anything like that. It's so silly."

Agnes fought to keep her anger under control. "Margaret believed in it. I felt it necessary since it was important to her."

"It's a nice gesture," Josephine said as she sat down. "Now, about that piano. Do you want it? Do you play?"

Agnes hung her head low. "No."

Timothy, Josephine's husband, sauntered into the room.

"Timothy! We were just discussing Margaret's piano."

"Did you want it?" He asked Agnes.

"She doesn't play, so she has no need of it." Josephine answered.

"We currently have no room in our house." He said. "Perhaps you could store it for us, until we are able to fit it into our parlor."

"Oh I'm sure she wouldn't mind. Would you, Agnes?"

"No," she responded quietly.

"I say we at least get it out of her way. I'm sure she doesn't need it taking up so much room in her house. Why don't you and Walter move it down cellar?"

"That would have to be another day since Walter is not with us." He replied.

"Oh that's no hassle at all." Josephine replied. She turned her attention to Agnes. "Why don't you go through Margaret's belongings and find something by which to remember her. Then, in a couple of days or so, we can come back, remove all of her belongings and personal items, and the men can move the piano down to your cellar. Isn't that just the perfect plan?"

Perfect? That plan was anything than perfect. It was selfish, materialistic, and hurtful at best. Sadly, Agnes had no recourse. She knew she had to agree to Josephine's wishes, even though it broke her heart. Finally, Agnes found the strength to speak. "Yes." She dejectedly responded.

"Wonderful! We will call on you again in a couple of days." Josephine stood up and left with Timothy.

As soon as she heard the door close, Agnes sat in front of the piano and wailed. She just lost Margaret: the person on whom she based her entire life. Now, she was going to lose the piano. The piano that she had purchased for Margaret. The gift that blessed them both was going to be placed down in the cellar where it would never see the light of day again.

Agnes slowly walked through the field. The field which used to be bigger. The field in which she and Chief would simply run away from all their cares and concerns. The field which was home to all the various critters she loved.

The sky was an amazing shade of azure blue. Only a few little clouds floated happily in the panoramic sky. The sun was bright and warm.

Today Agnes did not feel the warmth, though. The clouds did not entertain her. The field was void. Her cares and concerns walked with her.

Everything seemed so empty and meaningless now that Margaret was gone. The love of her life. Her best friend. Her partner. Her lover. Her confidant. The only person besides Chief who truly understood her. Margaret. Dear, sweet, beautiful, wonderful Margaret. No one at the funeral knew the depth of Agnes' loss. Sympathies had been extended, but even her own family did not mourn as soulfully as Agnes. No one understood. No one could possibly understand this kind of isolation and loneliness. Five horrific days have passed. Five seconds, five minutes, five hours, five days, five weeks, five months, five years. Time didn't matter. Nothing mattered. Everything was irrelevant without Margaret, and there was no escape from this pain.

Josephine walked right into the house. "Agnes!" She called out.

Agnes wearily walked out and saw her. "Hello, Josephine." She tried to feign some pleasantry.

"Timothy and Walter are on their way in to move the piano. Can you show me which room belonged to Margaret?"

Margaret's room. What a farce! They had always kept some clothes and a couple of photographs to make it seem as though Margaret held a separate room, but it was all just for show. People didn't understand them. People judged them harshly enough. If they were to know the true depth of their relationship, Agnes feared what might happen. They maintained this room specifically for times like this, but how Agnes hated this very sentiment and this very moment.

She quietly led Josephine to the room.

"Ah, perfect! Thank you." Josephine wasted no time in gathering Margaret's clothes. With her arms buried under countless dresses, Josephine walked out to the car and placed them in the trunk.

Agnes looked around the room one last time, knowing she was permanently losing the sights, smells and memories of Margaret. As she looked, she saw the jewelry box on the night stand. What a mistake! That was hers: it was a gift from Margaret. She must have placed it there accidentally as she was placing more items in the room for Josephine. Agnes quickly snatched it up.

Josephine came back all too quickly. She saw Agnes clutching the jewelry box to her chest.

Pianissimo

"Ah! Margaret's jewelry. I should take that as it has all of her personal jewelry as well as some family heirlooms." Josephine grabbed a hold of it.

Agnes did not lessen her grip. "I'm afraid..."

"Come on, give it to me now. I know you want something to remember her by, but this really should stay with the family."

In the background Agnes heard Timothy say, "One, two, three!" The men began pushing the piano through the house.

Agnes quickly whipped around to see the beautiful piano leaving its home of so many years.

Josephine pulled harder on the jewelry box. "This belongs to me!"

Agnes turned back towards Josephine. "No!" She shouted. She quickly realized what she had done; she quieted her voice. "Excuse me, please. But this is actually my jewelry box. It was a gift from Margaret, but the box and the jewelry inside are all my own. I must have accidentally placed it in here when I was cleaning last night. It is mine, though, not Margaret's."

Josephine retracted her arms. "Oh," she sneered. "Where is hers, then?"

Agnes took a deep breath. "It should be in here. Perhaps it is the drawer of her night table. Or perhaps it is on the dresser, or in one of the dresser drawers. I do not know as I don't go through her personal items."

Josephine's eyes narrowed and she looked angrily at Agnes.

Agnes slowly made her way out of the room.

Josephine could be heard as she quickly scrambled to get as much as she could. She began to leave and walk towards the car again. "Timothy!" She called out. "Are you almost done? I do think it's best that we leave right away."

Agnes heard the men continuing to push. Then she heard crashes, banging and keys screaming as the piano went tumbling down the stairs. After several large crashes, there was silence. An eerie, horrible silence.

Agnes walked to the window and watched the three of them pull away.

Still clutching the jewelry box to her chest, Agnes began to sob uncontrollably. She crumpled to the floor and wept.

Agnes paced around the bedroom. "Oh Margaret! Dear, sweet Margaret. I cannot tell you how awful these past few days have been. It has not even been a week, and yet it has felt like a lifetime. This is horrible."

She stopped and looked at herself in the mirror. "Losing my parents was hard. I came from a strong, stoic family, though. I grieved their passing, but life required that I press on.

"Losing Chief created a huge chasm in my soul. I had more years with him than I did my own parents. Before you, he was the only soul that understood me. He never passed judgment on me. He simply let me escape with him when we would race through the fields. He was a gentle giant. Losing him was tremendous."

Tears began to slowly roll down her high cheek bones. "Losing you, though," her voice cracked. "Has been the greatest devastation of my life. You who were God's special gift to me. You who were my best friend. You with whom I could share and trust my deepest, darkest secrets and fears. You who always stood by my side. You who taught me the definition of true love. You who were simply magical."

She cast her gaze on the floor. "I feel so empty. There is nothing inside me. No hope, no joy, no love, no life." She paused before starting to circle around the room again. "I do not understand why I am here. I cannot fathom any reason that I should still be alive without you. There is nothing here for me. Life holds no other promises or blessings. There is nothing awaiting me. I have waited and wondered why my heart would continue to beat without you. I have questioned God time and again, requesting an answer as to why I should breathe and you not."

She sat down on the bed and buried her face in her hands. "I do not understand, Margaret. It defies all logic that I should be without you. I cannot understand why I must endure this pain and these horrific minutes in solitude. What purpose could there be to this? What reason could possibly exist to explain this very moment? There is no purpose; there is no reason."

She dried the tears off her face. "There is nothing, Margaret. Nothing for me without you. I cannot live without you. I cannot exist without you. I need you. I need you here. I need to be with you."

"Then come with me."

It was a whisper. A whisper that only Agnes could hear, but it was clear as day. It was real. It was Margaret. There was no doubt in Agnes' mind. Margaret had spoken to her. Margaret was beckoning her to come join her in Heaven.

Why not? There was nothing left for Agnes. Only a quiet life of solitude and pain. A life without joy; a life without love.

"Yes!" Agnes exclaimed. "Yes Margaret, I will come to you! I will join you. I will be with you once again."

She inhaled deeply knowing it would be one of her last breaths. This was not a death she needed to incur on herself. She intuitively knew that her heart was simply going to stop sometime tonight. Yes. This was it. Relief, reprieve and reunion with her wonderful Margaret were coming soon. Agnes felt a peace come over her. Death did not frighten her – the thought of being brought together with Margaret again delighted her. This was her last night alone.

Suddenly a thought came to her.

"I must hide these!" Agnes whispered to herself.

She hurriedly grabbed an envelope and began stuffing it full of letters and pictures. No one was to know about these. She feared what could happen if anyone were to find out the true nature of her relationship with Margaret. She dared not let Josephine or anyone else in Margaret's family know. That would be horrendous. She would rather the townspeople didn't know either. It was simply better if it could be kept as a secret. They had faced such judgment, harassment, and discrimination as it was. They should both be allowed to maintain some form of dignity in death, at least. As long as she could keep all of these letters and photographs hidden, the secret would be buried with her.

She stuffed the last of the letters and photos into the very full envelope. Now, where to put it?

She went down into the cellar. Her heart stopped when she saw the once beautiful piano now dented and depreciated. It was shoved aside against the wall in a cellar with no light.

She didn't think Josephine or Timothy would come back for it. Besides, the house was hers. Once she died, they had no rights on the property. Perhaps it bravery to put it by the piano: she couldn't be sure that Josephine would never come back around. Perhaps it was sentimentality: to place her love letters by the one thing that meant the most to them both. Whatever the reason, Agnes put the envelope in an old hat box next to the piano.

Once that was all settled, she slowly climbed the stairs. She took one last long look at the piano, emblazing it in her memory.

She went back upstairs and climbed into bed, knowing she'd never see the sun rise again.

Corinne grabbed another photo.

There were Agnes and Margaret. Together. They stood next to each other. Their hair was all gathered and bunched on the tops of their heads, with dark, elegant hats sitting on top. Agnes wore a white shirt-waist blouse with puffy "leg o' mutton" sleeves tucked into a belt with a long dark skirt reaching the ground. Margaret wore a white, lacey dress. A ribbon with a large bow pulled the dress in at her waist, but then it flowed back down and hid her feet. They both wore polite smiles. They were each beautiful, and they were even more beautiful together. What a great picture.

Placing that one aside, Corinne reached for another photograph.

Agnes stood alone. She wore a long black dress and a big black hat. She normally stood regally. In this picture, she looked defeated. Her eyes looked dull and empty. Her vivaciousness was gone.

Corinne flipped the picture to see the back.

Agnes October 14, 1949.

Agnes, right after Margaret died. Clearly losing Margaret stole a large piece of Agnes' soul.

She reached into the envelope. There was one last newspaper cut out.

On Monday, October 17, 1949, Agnes Walker passed away from unknown causes. Miss Walker worked as a teacher at the primary school for over thirty years. She was the last descendent of Angus Walker, a Scottish Immigrant who became a prominent citizen in Louisville. Miss Walker has no survivors as she never married nor had any children. The Louisville School District will hold a service for her on Thursday, October 20.

Corinne figured the math in her head. 1949 minus 1887. Agnes was only sixty two. Sixty two. She was awfully young. Yes, people die young, but you don't hear about it often. Sixty two. Corinne couldn't imagine dying at that age.

"I wonder what she died from." She whispered.

Then it came to her. It was a thought, but it was almost as if someone had told her, "A broken heart." She lost her parents at a young age. She lost her beloved horse unexpectedly. And then she lost her Margaret. The one person who meant more to her than life itself. Agnes could not carry on any longer. The pain was far too great.

Corinne began placing everything back into the envelope.

"Wait a minute." She said out loud.

She looked down. All of the pictures, letters, and newspaper clippings had all been placed in that envelope by Agnes. She was the one who put it all together and hid it. No one had been in the house for twenty years, and since then, it doesn't look like anyone had touched it. It was right where Agnes had placed it: by the piano. But if that was the case, how on earth did her obituary get in there? She was dead, so she wasn't able to put it in herself. But no one else had touched the items in that box. Not since 1949. How was that possible? Who could have done that? Why? If they were going to add to Agnes' collection, wouldn't they have brought it to the town historian or something? That was weird. Really weird.

Corinne slowly placed everything back in the envelope. She was very disturbed by this thought. But there was no way she could ever truly know how the obituary got in there.

Chapter Twenty-One

Corinne was trying to find more information on Agnes on an ancestral, lineage, and heritage website when her computer notified her of an in-coming Skype call.

She didn't recognize it, but she answered anyway.

Suddenly, Darryl's face sat on her screen. His dark brown hair peeked out from under his camo cap. His dark brown eyes were warm and bright. His light brown skin looked fairly dark. His thin lips were cocked into a smirk. His wonderful, handsome face was right there. She wished she could just reach out and touch him. Was it a picture, like all of the pictures she had been staring at over these past months, or was it really him?

He blinked.

Corinne lost her breath. "Darryl?"

"Hey babe! How are you?"

Corinne was crying. "I...I don't know. You're there and you're alive, and..."

"And I'm coming home." He smiled.

"What? You are?! Oh my gosh! How? When? Why?"

Darryl laughed at her excitement. "They've started pulling troops out and our unit is one of the ones they're sending home."

Corinne squealed in excitement.

"We are leaving in two weeks. So, I should be back home in about seventeen to twenty one days."

"You are! You are coming home! In days! Just a matter of a few days! Oh that is wonderful! I cannot wait for you to come home!"

"I can't wait to be home. I need to get going for now, but I'll see you soon, okay?"

"Yes! I'll see you soon! I love you!"

Darryl's smile grew even bigger. "I love you too."

The reminder on her phone buzzed away. It was October seventeenth. She was a little nervous about doing this. She had only just put the finish on last week. Was it going to catch fire? Was it going to ruin all of her hard work? Corinne had no idea. She was going to try, though, and see what happened.

With two tea light candles, her phone, and a lighter in hand, she walked down the creaky old steps into the basement.

She placed her phone on the dryer. She placed the two tea light candles on both ends of the top of the piano. She started the lighter and lit them up.

"It's October seventeenth, Agnes." Corinne said. "It's the anniversary of the day you died. It's been a long time – a really long time since you died, though.

"I know this was important to you and Margaret. I kinda figured no one lit any candles for you, so I thought I would do it today, if that's okay."

Corinne began pacing the room. "I must sound crazy, walking around here talking to myself. Can you even hear me, Agnes? Do you know that I'm here?" She paused. "I guess it's better to be crazy and weird than disrespectful and not doing anything to acknowledge you. Right?

"I'm sorry these aren't like the candles you used to burn. It's just that since I just put the new finish on it and the ventilation is so poor down here, I wanted to be careful. Better to be safe than sorry, right?"

She turned and looked directly at the piano. "Speaking of the finish, what do you think? Do you like how the piano looks? Do you think I did an okay job? I'm sure it doesn't look nearly as good as when you bought it for Margaret, but it looks nice. At least I think so."

She began pacing around the room again. "I worked really hard on it. Really hard. It was tough. There was so much paint and junk and missing boards. This was not an easy project at all. I think I'm glad I did it, though. I really got to learn a lot and now look! I can continue to play the same piano Margaret played." She stopped.

"Oh! I never thought to ask. Is that okay that I'm playing the same piano as Margaret? I know she's the only one who ever played it. I never even thought to ask permission, but is it okay? I didn't mean to be disrespectful. I was just trying to help."

Corinne decided to sit down on the cold, hard basement floor. "I'm sorry I can't bring the piano back upstairs. Even before I started to work on it, it was obvious that it would cause more damage to try to haul it up here somehow. I'm sorry. I'm still going to play it, though. It won't be a concert hall; it won't even really be for guests. But I'll play it down here. For me, and maybe even for you two."

Corinne danced her long, thin fingers all around herself on the floor. "Do you remember little Rich Adams? Lacy's son? He lives in her house now. He says he remembers both of you. He seems to be a lot nicer than his mother ever was to you. He's a nice guy. He's helped me out with this a lot. It was really neat being able to talk to him and have him tell me his memories of you. I know they weren't much. He was really young when you both died, but you still made a lasting impression! I thought that was cool."

Corinne's eyes rose from the floor to back up at the piano. "I know what it's like to be alone, Agnes. I mean, my parents didn't die when I was young or anything. But my husband, Darryl, is in the Army. And he's gone for months at a time. This most recent tour will be a total of sixteen months. Can you believe that? Sixteen long, lonely months. I hate it." Corinne sighed. "I just wanted you to know you have my sympathy. I know what it's like. It's the worst feeling in the world."

Corinne stood up again and stretched. "I don't want to leave. Not until the candles burn out. I don't want there to be any problems, you know?"

She gently placed a finger on one of the keys. "Margaret, if you're here too, I've been trying to take care of your piano for you. See? I'm being very gentle and careful with it. Do you like it? Do you think I did a good job?"

She yawned. She never imagined burning tea light candles would take so long! Corinne began walking around again.

"No offense, but I hope these candles burn out soon. I don't know much how longer I can just hang out down here. It's nothing against you. It's just cold, dark and dirty down here."

She took a deep breath. "I know I've never met you and I never will, but in seeing all of those pictures, reading the letters, the newspaper articles and your diary, Agnes, has really changed things a lot for me. I've never known anyone who was gay before. I never really gave it much thought. It wasn't my cup of tea. I always thought gay people were kind of weird. I figured as long as they didn't bother me, I wouldn't bother them. But that was it. I didn't 'support' it or anything. I always took more of a 'hands-off' approach to things like that.

"But now I see that you're no different than me and Darryl. You two loved each other. You went through a lot of stuff together and that Clarence guy treated you like dirt! You guys went through good times and bad. It wasn't easy. But you were both so dedicated to each other. It wasn't about loving a gender, it was about loving a person. And you did. You both loved each other very much."

She paused for a moment. "I'll tell you what. A lot of couples today could learn so much from you guys. People nowadays get divorced at the drop of a hat. Now, people don't have nearly the same struggle you two had, and yet they give up far too easily! I guess..." She waited. "If there was anything I could say to you it's thank you. Thank you for leaving all of these gifts so I could find out about you. Thank you for loving each other, and living such a great life together. And thank you for teaching me that love is love."

In perfect unison, both candles perfectly burned out. Small swirls of smoke rose up towards Heaven. Perhaps they had heard Corinne all along.

Rich inspected the piano very closely. "Wow! It's all done, Corinne. You've done it!"

She smiled. "We've done it. There was no way I would have been able to do this without your help. I really cannot tell you how much I appreciate it."

"It's been my pleasure. It's been fun getting to know you and going through the history of the house and piano."

"Speaking of that, there's something I need to tell you." Corinne wrinkled her face. She was so afraid as to how he'd react. Did she really have to tell him? No. But now it was too late. She had started the conversation, there was no going back.

"Yeah?" Rich asked.

"Rich, the reason they were loners and not really liked was because..." Oh geez! How could she tell him this? It could hurt him – and she certainly did not have the words to put it all together. She hesitated.

"Because?"

She hemmed and hawed. Finally, she spoke. "Because they were gay. They were lesbians living together. They never got married because they couldn't get married – to each other." She winced.

Rich changed his stance. "Really?"

"Yeah," she reluctantly answered him.

"Well that explains a lot. People back then couldn't understand it. It was completely unacceptable at that time."

"Yeah it was. They had a great life together, but they were treated like dirt because of who they were."

"You know, I'm not really a big fan. Call me old fashioned. But I don't think it was right that they were ostracized the way they were. Just live and let live. But too many people can't leave well enough alone. They always have to have their noses in other people's business."

"Yeah. It's sad."

"I agree. Hopefully they're in a better place and they're more accepted now." He briefly paused. "Well, the important part is that you got that piano all finished. It looks great!"

Corinne smiled. "It sure does. Thank you again!"

"No problem. Enjoy!"

Rich smiled before walking away.

Well, he took that fairly well, she thought. It could have been better, but it could have been worse. Way worse. Now he knew the deep dark secret that went with them to the grave. It didn't lessen their talents or humanity. They were still good women. Good women who deserved to be respected and remembered. Good women whose memories he and Corinne would carry with them always.

"Hey!" Rachel said cheerfully. It had been a while since they last talked. She certainly sounded friendlier.

"Hi," Corinne said weakly.

"How are you doing?"

"Good, good. I've been busy."

"Oh yeah? Doing what?"

"Do you remember me telling you about the piano in the basement."

"Hmmmm." Rachel took a few moments to think and recall. "Yeah, vaguely."

"Well, I've been restoring it."

"You've been restoring a piano? When did you learn how to do that?"

"It's pretty simple, really. I've just been sanding and refinishing the wood. I've had to buy some wood to replace certain parts. But that's all done now. I just finished fixing the keys, and now I just need to get it tuned."

"Since when did you know how to do all this? How do you know so much about pianos?"

"I played the piano for like twelve years."

"You did?"

"Yeah. Besides, it's been fun learning how to do this. And I've been learning about the house's history."

"What do you mean?"

"I stumbled upon an old box with pictures, articles, journals all kinds of neat stuff about the family that built the house, the people that have lived here over the years. It's really kind of cool."

"Do you still think the house is haunted?"

"Yeah, but it's just the girls."

"The girls? I thought the girls were your cats."

"They are. I have the kitty girls and the people girls. So yes, they're the girls. That's what I call them. Agnes and Margaret."

"So they're sisters?"

"No."

"No?" Rachel asked.

"No. They're...lesbians."

Rachel laughed hardily. "You have gay ghosts?"

Corinne paused. "Yes," she answered quietly.

"So you're not even sure you believe in ghosts. That was until now. And you don't have regular ghosts. You have gay ghosts. How do you feel about that?"

"I don't know. It's okay, I guess."

"Are they hitting on you?" Rachel roared with laughter.

"No!" Corinne defended them. "They're actually very sweet. They love each other. I've never seen two people more in love. It's really changed how I see gay people."

Rachel coughed. "Seriously?"

"Yes!" Corinne huffed. "Anyway, Agnes likes animals and Margaret plays the piano."

"She plays the piano?"

"Yeah."

"She actually plays the piano?"

"Yes!" Corinne shouted.

"Okay. Sorry."

"She plays the piano. It's her piano. It's Agnes' house. And they live here. They lived here, and they're still here now."

"Huh. Okay."

"So it's their house. And Agnes plays with the cats and Margaret plays the piano."

"Okay. And what's the problem? They sound like nice ghosts."

"They are." Corinne agreed.

"Hey, at least you have company now!"

Corinne was silent.

Pianissimo

"Come on! I'm just trying to cheer you up. Geez, Corinne. Sometimes I think this move was the worst thing that ever happened to you."

"Me too," Corinne whispered before hanging up.

Corinne vacuumed again and again. She wanted the house to be spotless. She had dusted everything three times, and now she was vacuuming making sure she was getting all of the fallen dust, cat hair and whatever else may have fallen on the floor.

She cleaned the mirror in the bathroom. She scrubbed the sink tirelessly. She sprayed down the shower with a spray foam cleaner and then washed it all away with scalding hot water. She cleaned and polished the toilet bowl until it looked brand new.

She walked through every room three times. He was going to be home very soon. She wanted the house to be absolutely perfect.

She found one of their wedding pictures and shifted it so that it sat perfectly on the shelf. Just as soon as she released her hand, she heard the door open.

"Hello?" His warm, deep, sensual, wonderful voice filled the house.

Corinne ran out and jumped on him, holding him as tightly as she could.

"Hi, babe." He chuckled. He gently put her down and looked deeply into her eyes.

"I can't believe you're here! You're finally home. And you're going to stay home. You're not going to leave any more! You're here with me!"

He smiled. "Yes I am. I know you like the idea now, but you'll be sick of me in no time!"

She hugged him tightly again. "No I won't! Not ever. I am so happy you're here. I love you!"

"I love you too, babe. Want to show me our new house?"

"Yes!" She exclaimed. "Yes, yes, yes! Come with me!" She grabbed his hand and began to run through the house. "C'mon, c'mon! Let me show you!" She squealed with excitement.

"Hold on! Let me look." Darryl looked around the kitchen. It was really cute. He nodded his head showing he approved. "Nice job, babe."

"Thanks! But that's not what I want to show you."

"I finally get to live in my new house and you don't even want to show me what it looks like or what you've done?" He laughed.

"You'll see it every day! I want to show you my big project."

"You had a big project? And what was that?"

"Come on, let me show you!"

She brought him to the cellar door and nudged it open with her hip. "It's right down here."

They made their way down the stairs.

She turned on the dim basement light.

"There it is!" She beamed with pride.

Darryl turned to see the piano.

"A piano? What was so big about this?"

"Oh! You should have seen it. It had cobwebs all over. Keys were stuck and broken. It was painted green."

"It was green?"

Corinne nodded. "Yeah. Uh huh."

"Okay? Why was it green, and why is there a piano in the basement?"

"We don't know who painted. Rich thinks..."

"Who's Rich?" He cut her off.

"That's our neighbor across the street. Rich and Susie. Really nice folks. Anyway, Rich thinks that some stupid college kids painted it green when this was being used for student housing."

Darryl's face contorted into an expression of utter confusion. "What?"

"Oh, it's a whole long story, I'll tell you later. Anyway, the piano was here when we bought the house. It was moved down here in 1949."

"How the hell do you know all this?"

"Like I said, it's a really long story; don't worry about that now. The point is: it was green, it was missing pieces – it was a God awful wreck. It was built in 1907, and has been here ever since. So one day, I decided to see if I could fix it. I started sanding it. And then Rich let me borrow his Dremmel. He helped me cut wood slabs to replace the missing pieces."

Darryl looked at her. "You did all this? With our neighbor?"

"Yeah! He was great. He taught me a lot."

"Okay...?"

"So he helped me, and we fixed it. Completely. Sanded, finished, fixed – completely restored and working again!"

Darryl took a step back. "Wow! Babe, I'm impressed. I never thought you knew how to use power tools."

"I didn't before this. But man is it fun!"

Darryl smirked. "Yup." He started to look the piano over. He walked all around it. "So why isn't it upstairs?"

"Rich and I both thought we could do more damage by trying to get it back up, so we figured it would be better staying down here."

"And what are we going to do with it?"

"I've started playing again."

Darryl's spun around; his eyes were huge. "You have?"

Corinne smiled brightly. "Yeah!"

"That's awesome! Good for you!" He pulled her in close. "I am so proud of you. You fixed up our new house really nice. You took on a big project all by yourself. Now you know how to use power tools. And you started playing again. That is awesome, babe. It really is."

She looked up at him. "Thanks."

Corinne curled in close to Daryl. Her nose rested at the nape of his neck. She inhaled deeply. It was real; it was him. His scent. This was perfection. She wrapped her arms around his stomach, making sure he could never leave her again. She easily slipped into that wonderful dreamy between being awake, and being completely asleep. Gentle piano music lulled her to sleep.

"What is that?" Daryl jerked and jumped up. He ran to the bedroom door and opened it. "Corinne, do you hear that? What is that?"

"Oh," she yawned. "That's nothing. Come back to bed."

"It's nothing? Where the hell is that piano music coming from?"

Corinne yawned again. "It's nothing. Don't worry about it. It's just the girls."

Book Club Discussion Starters

Pianissimo

by Lauren Shiro

- Who are Millie and Mollie? What is their importance to Corinne?

- The story opens with a raging storm just outside of Corinne and the new, empty house. What does that storm signify?

- What is your take on the nature of Corinne's relationship with Rachel, and how that friendship evolves throughout the story?

- Who is David Butler? What does he contribute to the story?

- The piano is painted a "drab, olive green" color. Corinne likens it to her husband's Army fatigues. What do you believe is the connection or symbolism between the two?

- At first, Corinne tells Bob that she has no interest in restoring the piano. She later decides to tackle the project herself. What do you think caused that change of heart?

- Of all of the ways Corinne connects with Margaret and Agnes (love letters, photos, diary entries, etc.), which is your favorite and why?

- Who is Rich and what role does he play in Corinne's life?

- Who or what do you think was the biggest offender or obstacle in Agnes and Margaret's life?

- What does Chief symbolize or represent for Agnes?

- Corinne has very different experiences with sales people at the hardware store, the lumber yard, and finally Kevin with the paints and stains. What are your thoughts on these different experiences and their significances?

- What does the burning down of the original home signify, or does it even signify anything?

- What does the title, *Pianissimo,* reference?

- Darryl finally comes back to a new home, and in a way, a new Corinne. He seems to take it all in stride. Are you surprised by this? Why or why not?

- Was this more of a paranormal story, an historical account, a tale of personal growth, or a saga of forbidden love? Why?

More Books by Lauren Shiro

Loving Her, Volume 1
by Lauren Shiro

In this series of stories, we meet a group of loving friends and couples. Each member of this group is diverse in personalities and abilities, but they are tied together by the common denominator - love.

from Chelle Cordero, Combining Passion & Suspense

This volume contains the first four stories in the Loving Her series. Each is also available as individual short stories. Loving Her, Volume 1 is coming soon in audio, and is available in print and all electronic editions.

Book 1
The Ballerina

A southern, redheaded, pickup driving lesbian ballerina? You bet! Meet Liz: a southern belle with flair. Vivacious, eclectic and graceful, she is unique to say the least. The first in the series of Loving Her stories, Liz's story is the kind that stays with you long after you've closed the book.

Book 2
The Cop

Donna White is one tough cop. Behind the badge, though, is a very sweet, sad, sensitive soul. Truly a woman alone, Donna is simply trying to navigate her way through life. Who is Donna? She is dedicated, determined, distinctive and deep. Donna's rich and touching story is second in the Loving Her series.

Book 3
The Mechanic

Linda - her name means beautiful... After facing rejection from her parents because she is a lesbian, Linda didn't feel beautiful... she felt lost and alone. As a skilled mechanic, Linda built her business... Her love life was a different matter. Until Katie... They survived the brutal beatings they received at the hands of Katie's ultra-religious father. Together they survived, and together would face their future, and find hope and a joy neither expected.

Book 4
The Model

She's exotic. She's beautiful. She's talented. She's unique. She's Stephania. A young successful model who started from nothing, she has experienced all the ups and downs of life. Never one to be kept down, she persists through life's trials and reaches for the fairytale ending she has always hoped for. Stephania's emotional journey is the fourth story in the Loving Her series.

Loving Her, Volume 2
by Lauren Shiro

In this series of stories, we meet a group of loving friends and couples. Each member of this group is diverse in personalities and abilities, but they are tied together by the common denominator - love. from Chelle Cordero, Combining Passion & Suspense ...

Volume 2 includes: The Peace Officer, The Shelter Director, The Writer, and The Vet Student

Book 5
The Peace Officer

Brynn Racanelli - daughter, sister, friend, partner, police officer... and so much more. Devoted to serving others through her police work, and to helping her sister who battles chronic Lyme Disease, she is the the poster child of selflessness. But she does have wants, needs, hopes, and dreams. Will fate finally bring her the life and love she's always dreamed of?

Book 6
The Shelter Director

Shy, quiet, humble – Jen is the kind of person that would give you the shirt off her back and then ask you what else you need. She may not be a movie star, but she'll treat you like one. She works diligently to help save cats. She sacrifices her life and stability to accommodate her partner. She gives until it hurts, and her reward is a devastating diagnosis. What will her life become?

Book 7
The Writer

Everyone has that one friend; the mother of the group. Maria is that one friend; nurturing, wise, and with a spicy streak, Maria is the matriarch of the clan. Cerebral, emotional, and even sometimes comical, Maria's story is the seventh in the Loving Her series.

Book 8
The Vet Student

Determined to escape the small town and her religious, stifling parents,Katie works hard to get into veterinary school... in Philadelphia. Katie refused to let anything – or anyone – destroy her dream. Not even her own parents. She suffered many losses along the way, but she gained so much more. Tumultuous and tender, Katie's story closes the Loving Her series... for now.

NOVELS

Unbreakable Hostage

Lareina Oliveira; she wants to share her passion for math. So it is back to school for Lareina... a tough Ph.D. program. A classmate is captivated by Lareina's beauty and intelligence, and despite her repeated refusals to his attentions, he kidnaps her! Only her determination and wits can save her...

Imperfect

Carol Mathers, in her mid-thirties, a highly sought-after IT guru in St. Louis. She has built a great life for herself with her partner, Alexandria, even though the two face prejudice as lesbians, and as an interracial couple - fighting tragedy and sometimes, triumphing amidst the chaos...

Impeccable

Carol – abandoned - waiting... for what, she couldn't know. She couldn't see that there was more life waiting for her. Carol is forced to face the demons of her past as well as begin to face life without Alex. Struggling to make sense of it all, Carol experiences her new life and all of the highs and lows that come with that life.

Short Stories

Amnesie, a short story

What happens to love when life changes? Two women in love, one debilitating change...

Trajectory, a short story

Joe Davis has spent the last four years of his life behind a scope as a sniper for the Detroit PD's SWAT Team. A fateful call sends Joe and his team deep into the Detroit Ghetto; and reminds him that there is more to life than what's on the other end of his gun.

Lauren Shiro
Love without Boundaries

In celebration of her one year wedding anniversary and recent political changes that legalize her marriage, author Lauren E. Harvey (L. E. Harvey) and Vanilla Heart Publishing are excited to announce the re-releases of her books and a brand new series of Loving Her singles under her (legal) married name,
Lauren Shiro.

Lauren Shiro was published nationally for the first time at age fourteen. Since then, her work has been published in newspapers, magazines, literary journals, and even textbooks.

In 2006, she began writing fiction and she hasn't stopped yet. From her set of intertwined short stories in *Loving Her*, to the powerhouse duo of *Imperfect* and *Impeccable*, Lauren has written stories that are sure to touch your heart. Lauren continues to write stories of love without boundaries.

When she's not writing, Lauren works as a licensed veterinary technician. In her spare time, she enjoys everything from wood working to roller derby. She resides in Rochester, New York with her wife and their menagerie of furry and feathered friends.

Visit with Lauren
Email AuthorLaurenShiro@gmail.com
Facebook Facebook.com/LaurenShiro77
Twitter twitter.com/AuthorLShiro @authorlshiro
Blog LaurenShiro.blogspot.com
Website LaurenShiro.com

www.ingramcontent.com/pod-product-compliance
Lightning Source LLC
Chambersburg PA
CBHW070813120626
46556CB00002B/483